Praise ~~for the Bestselling New Adult~~
romance, I Found You

"Jane Lark has proved what a writing talent she really is.
This is an engrossing and telling read…. Be prepared to
have your heart squeezed!"
BestChicklit.com

"An amazing book. It is dark and edgy yet flirtatious and
even made me laugh. It's such a combination that made
me not want to put my kindle down at all."
After the Final Chapters

"Dark, gritty and wholly mesmerizing, I Found You is a
haunting and compelling read you will not easily forget!"
Bookish Jottings

"Emotional, romantic, and heartbreaking."
Imagine a World

JANE LARK

I love writing authentic, passionate and emotional love stories.

I began my first novel, a historical, when I was sixteen, but life derailed me a bit when I started suffering with Ankylosing Spondylitis, so I didn't complete a novel until after I was thirty when I put it on my to do before I'm forty list.

Now I love getting caught up in the lives and traumas of my characters, and I'm so thrilled to be giving my characters life in others' imaginations, especially when readers tell me they've read the characters just as I've tried to portray them.

You can follow me on Twitter @Jane Lark or find me on Facebook www.facebook.com/Janelarkauthor.

Just You

JANE LARK

Harper
impulse
we've got the love

Harper*Impulse* an imprint of
HarperCollins*Publishers* Ltd
77–85 Fulham Palace Road
Hammersmith, London W6 8JB

www.harpercollins.co.uk

A Paperback Original 2014

First published in Great Britain in ebook format by Harper*Impulse* 2014

A catalogue record for this book
is available from the British Library

ISBN: 9780008119478

Automatically produced by Atomik ePublisher from Easypress

Chapter One

Portia

My head hurt. It was like someone was firing a nail gun into the back of my skull. I must have drunk buckets last night.

The weight of my forearm lay on my forehead. I opened my eyes. I could see the sky through the skylight. The day was bleak. Gray. Miserable. Like I felt.

Memories flashed through my thoughts as if someone had switched a PowerPoint presentation running in my head, just images popping up, then sliding out. Shit. Justin. I sat up and my brain rolled forward like a ball of rock, hitting my skull... I felt ill.

I held still for a moment. I was going to throw up. I dived out of bed racing for the bathroom.

It was on days like this I missed people. Anyone. It would just be nice to have someone around who gave a shit sometimes.

Ten minutes later, with an empty belly, and a brain that didn't belong to me, I came out of the bathroom and headed for the sink by the burner. I poured myself a glass of water, then reached to get some Advil from the cupboard beside it to kill my headache. I drank some of the water, swallowed the pills and then washed them down with more water. My brain throbbed steadily, still protesting about the amount of alcohol I'd drunk the night before.

I sat on the bed, with my feet on the floor, and let memories and images, play through my head. *Oh my God.* I tumbled back, lying across the mattress, with my hands gripping my forehead and partly covering my eyes—as if I could hide from the pictures, like a stupid kid playing peek-a-boo. The images kept telling me the things I'd done.

Shit.

Did I have sex with Justin?

I didn't even like Justin like that.

"Oh my God, Portia. What have you done now?" I could remember him kissing me. I'd definitely kissed him. It was after we'd got in the pool. Jason had just disappeared. It was Jason my lonely brain had been interested in for weeks, though the guy was unavailable…

But Justin…

He wasn't bad looking, but he was no Jesse Williams, and he was a joker, and a bit of a douche. He always hung around the girls at work, too much—so much it was kind of creepy. He was one of those guys who worked so hard at being nice it made you want to back away…

More images paraded in my head. We'd gone through all the clothes and stuff in Mr. Rees's room looking for bikinis to wear in the pool… Yes, I had definitely been wearing one because there was an image in my head of his fingers slipping it aside to touch my breasts, and I could feel his fingers touching me too.

Shit. I shut my eyes, then opened them again as more pictures piled in.

His hand had been in my bottoms.

My palm gripped my forehead. When would I learn not to drink so much? Well it was January 1st; the day for resolutions.

I think I'd suggested looking for the pool too, but there had been four of us in it, not just me and Justin. It had been us and the other girls we sat near in the office, Crystal and Becky. Surely I wouldn't have let him do stuff if the others were there. Please tell me, even out of my head, I had better morals than that.

His friend Jason had been locked in the bathroom earlier in the night, during the part of the night I could remember, I'd offered to go in there and hung around to talk to him on the terrace later while he'd texted someone. That was when he'd reminded me it was his "*wife*" he was texting.

I had to give up alcohol—it made my judgment too bad.

Shit. I bet Justin just spotted an easy chance.

I sat up again, reaching for my cell. There was only one way I was going to find out. I flicked up the messages, then texted: 'Hey Becky. Happy New Year's! Is your head as bad as mine? What the hell did I do last night?' I tapped send on the text praying it wouldn't come back with a hideous acknowledgement that, yes, I'd entertained them in the pool with a live porn show. But they'd have stopped us long before his hand had got in my bikini bottoms, wouldn't they?

I had obviously been too drunk to stop it myself though.

My cell vibrated in my hand.

'Happy New Year's! We left before you. You were with Justin in the pool. I don't know. What did you do? ;)'

'Not much then probably. But I don't remember.'

'You'll have to ask Justin?'

'Think I'll pass.'

I threw my cell on the bed beside me. I couldn't even remember how I got home. Let alone if I got dressed after getting out the pool—and what did we do with the wet swimming stuff. Mr. Rees didn't even know we'd snuck into the pool. My dad would go psycho if someone had done that in his house. Maybe that's why my subconscious had thrown the idea in when I was drunk.

Maybe that was why I'd got in too deep with Justin—pay back. My dad would hate that too.

But why did I have to do it at the work party? That was really going to impress my boss. What if I'd stumbled back into his living room wearing his girlfriend's bikini, dripping water, and puked on his polished marble floor?

I'd get the pointed finger tomorrow. *You're fired.*

Dad would go super crazy if I told him I'd done something so embarrassing. He'd think it would impact on his reputation.

But I wasn't telling him because I wasn't going to lose my job, there would be a way to convince Mr. Rees to keep me on, if I had to. I'd worked out a hundred wiles for manipulating people in my years of growing up.

British boarding schools were full of stuck-up—get me I'm rich—bitches. You learned to be loud and stand up for yourself or you ended up the school dupe, laughed at and constantly bullied. I had got loud and I'd learned to win attention. Manipulation was an art I'd learned from my daddy though, not just school. But I wasn't proud of that.

Well, New Year's Day or not, it seemed to me the miserable weather, and my hangover, called for a day spent in bed watching any movie that didn't take much brain power to follow it. I leaned over and picked up my laptop, then lay back down and flipped the lid open.

I went into Netflix, ignoring Twitter and Instagram, and everything else. I didn't want to face any malicious office party pictures; I'd deal with them tomorrow. Today, I was all for pulling the bed covers over my head and hiding.

I scanned through the lists.

Justin

Fuck. My head felt like someone was banging it against a wall. Fucking free champagne. I wished I hadn't indulged so aggressively. But then, hey—it was free.

An image of Portia flowed into my head—Portia in an emerald green bikini. All the girls had looked hot, but she'd looked the best, and she'd felt pretty hot in the pool too—when the others had gone.

Shit. My head.

"Justin! Justin!" My eight-year-old kid brother rushed into my room, thrusting the door aside, and then jumped on my bed. My head spun, and my belly did a full roll, as pain pierced through my forehead and out the back of my skull like someone fired a gun through it.

"Go steady—you pain in the butt."

"It's New Year's, Mom's cooking lunch, it'll be ready soon. You're lazy."

"Cheers bro, but—get off, Dillon."

He climbed off me with a huge grin and then ran away again.

"You getting up, man?" I looked up. Another of my brothers, Robin, stood in the doorway, his shoulder resting against the doorjamb.

We shared this room, but he looked like he'd been up and dressed for ages.

Robin was seventeen. Then there was Jake who was fourteen.

"You were in late last night."

"Yeah." I sat up. My brain rolled around in my head like a pinball. I needed food and coffee. I pulled my T-shirt on.

"Mom's checked your cell."

"Great. I'm twenty-two, why the fuck is she checking my cell?"

"For the same reason you check ours. 'Cause she don't want you getting into trouble."

"Like I'd have a chance."

Robin twisted his lips in a grin that mocked me. I screwed up my face at him, saying *whatever*, as I stood and pulled my jeans on over my boxers, then ran my fingers over my hair.

"You look fucked."

"Don't copy my bad language. Mum 'll smack you 'round the ear for it. Do as I say, not as I do…" But I wished I had got fucked last night. Nearly.

I got another twisted smile.

Robin had grown out of idolizing me long ago, but we still got on, and we talked a lot, about everything. He rarely talked to Mom. But I kept him talking to me 'cause I didn't want him falling in

5

with any of the gangs in our neighborhood.

I think if he did have any trouble, he'd tell me.

I did look out for them, my brothers. All my brothers.

When I walked into the kitchen, I saw my cell on the counter next to Mom. She was mashing potatoes to go with the chicken that stood on the side. Lunch smelt good, spicy. My belly rolled over—hunger giving it a bite. That was all I needed to cure my hangover—food.

"Justin." Mom looked up at me turning her cheek.

I leaned down and kissed it. "Morning, Mom."

"Afternoon," she corrected, "And where were you, child?"

I rolled my eyes. "At Mr Rees's party, like I was last New Year's Eve. I told you where I was going. I told you I'd be late."

I knew why she was asking—for the same reason I checked up on Robin, Jake, and Dillon. 'Cause she didn't want me caught up in trouble—but she ought to know, I looked after myself. I'd got to twenty-two and stayed out of it.

"Mom, give me a little line, I'm not a kid. Trust me why don't you…"

She smiled, still smashing the potatoes. I caught up my cell and shoved it in my back pocket.

Jake was sitting on the sofa watching Dillon's cartoons, with his arms crossed over his chest. He was in a bad mood—but then the kid was always in a bad mood. It was a rite of passage for boys his age to be shitheads. A rite I hadn't had chance to claim. But Robin had gone through it and come out the other side… I had my fingers crossed for Jake.

He didn't talk to me much, but he talked to Robin. I figured if I kept Robin safe, Robin would do the same for Jake.

I hoped.

Mom started dishing up. "Wash up and sit at the table."

Dillon ran off to the bathroom to wash his hands, and Robin followed, to check he did it. Jake didn't move.

"Come on." Mom urged. She turned with a pile of cutlery in

her hand. I took it from her and laid it out on the table. Jake still hadn't moved as Dillon and Robin came back.

I glanced over my shoulder at him. He was staring at the TV. Dillon sat down and Robin moved to collect the plates, as Mom finished them off with corn. Jake still hadn't moved. I went over and knocked his leg with mine. He looked up.

With my gaze and a nod of my head I told him to *get the fuck up, asshole.* Mom worked hard for us. She'd been on her own for years, since before Dillon was born, but we'd never gone hungry or not had clothes. She deserved respect—even if she was like a bloody stalker some times.

I wasn't gonna lie and say it didn't annoy me. It annoyed me.

But she was like that because Dad had messed her around for years. He was a waster, a woman beater and a drug addict. She'd kicked him out when I was a little kid. He'd been released from jail for the fifth time, and when he'd crawled back and knocked on our door she'd pointed a finger at him and told him where to go, then slammed the door in his face.

Now her single-minded mission in life was that none of us would turn out like him.

That's why I gave her leeway 'cause out of all of us, I was the one who knew most about the things Dad had said and done.

For the last few years I'd spent my life trying to make it all up to her, and make her life easy—and that was why I was on the same mission as her—to make sure my brothers stayed out of trouble—and turned out nothing like the man who's DNA ran in our blood.

Jake moved, finally, 'cause he knew I was getting pissed off, and there was no point in messing with me. I'd lose my shit if he pissed me off.

I wasn't letting any of my brother's grow up like Dad. I didn't accept any of their bullshit. At least Robin had hit the point that he understood that. Jake? I didn't know about Jake… He was the odd one out, but only 'cause he was at that obnoxious teen stage.

He didn't know any better. It was just instinct at his age to think of himself first.

I wished I'd had that chance.

Chapter Two

Justin

When I walked into the office my gaze honed in on Portia. She was sitting at her desk, with earphones in, typing up some dictation. Or maybe listening to her latest favorite song and pretending to type up dictation—I knew she did that. I walked past her. She didn't acknowledge me, but I caught the color of her skin shifting up several levels of pink.

I smiled. Maybe if I'd been looking in a mirror it would have come out looking leery, but she didn't look up at me, just stared at her screen, like two days ago her tongue hadn't been in my mouth, and my fingers…

I walked over to the rack to strip off my jacket. Was she embarrassed about hooking up with me?

I turned and looked at her again. She was still staring at her screen with her fingers flying over the keyboard, but her face was nearly as red as the takeaway Starbucks cup sitting by her elbow. I wanted to laugh.

It looked like she was feeling awkward.

I wasn't suffering. I had no complaints. I was super happy with the opportunity she'd given me… The girl was awesome, if a bit arrogant. But, shit, I'd never really had any expectation I could hook up with a pretty, money loaded, white girl like Portia.

On my way back, I swiped the usual no-nonsense ponytail she had her blonde hair confined in. One of her hands lifted off the keyboard. But then it fell and she didn't look around.

Whenever I saw her outside work, her hair was always down. It had been down New Year's Eve.

Her pretty red lip-gloss painted mouth, that had a natural perfect pout, stayed closed. Her lips were held tightly together as she focused on her screen, like her screen was the savior of the world.

She was hiding from me, without actually hiding. She didn't want to face up to what had happened at the party. Clearly she *did* regret our little interlude.

Well, whatever. Who gave a shit?

I sat down—ignoring her too.

If that's the way she wanted to play it—that's the way we'd play it.

I had two pages of the magazine to pull together today. Vacations always had to be paid for, I'd be short of time today.

My mate Jason rocked up twenty minutes after me, just before nine, drawing a fine line between being on time and getting caught up in a pile of shit; especially as he'd had a bunch of time off with short notice before Christmas.

He threw his stuff down under the desk and glared at his computer, starting it up. He seemed in just as bad a mood as Portia.

"Where'd you go to New Year's Eve, you just disappeared?"

"I had to go." He looked up at me. "Rach texted." That didn't have a ring of truth, it stunk of an excuse.

"Wife-y got you on a ball and chain already?" The guy had got married about a week ago. I mean he was twenty-two and the girl was already knocked up, and he'd only met her two months ago. *Fool.* But then I'd never seen the girl, maybe she was *that* hot.

My screen pinged to say I'd got an email.

'Can we get a coffee at lunchtime?' It was from Portia.

I glanced over at her desk, but I couldn't see anything other than her arm.

'Okay. What time?'

'12.30. Meet me in Starbucks.'

'Ashamed of me, baby?'

There was no reply. I had a feeling the conversation was gonna go something like—*don't tell anyone I hooked up with you.*

Well we were from different leagues. The girl was arrogant and preppy and she liked to stick her pretty little nose up in the air.

Her tastes had turned to Jason, she'd had her eye on him for weeks. Me... I was just the one who'd been there when she'd got drunk... When she was sober—I was way below her standards.

I said something about the party to Jason. He ignored me and glanced at Mr. Rees's office. The boss wasn't in yet.

Jason looked over to the door into the office.

I gave up trying to talk and focused on getting my pages done. The whole place was in a bad mood today.

At eleven-thirty, not that I was clock checking, Portia got up and headed for the restrooms. She was slender, but she was slender with hips. The girl had some junk in her trunk for sure, Beyoncé style, and she had a pencil skirt on today that exaggerated the movement of her hips as she walked across the open plan room weaving between desks. The movement thrust the image of her ass in an emerald bikini into my head. My temperature soared.

I got up, without even thinking about it—and followed.

When I got in there, I found myself hovering outside the women's like a pervert.

I leaned against the wall, slipping my hands into the back pockets of my pants.

She took a couple of minutes to come out, but when she did her pretty pouted lips parted in an 'o' and she turned pink... tipping up her chin, and her pretty little nose, with a look that implied disgust, like I smelled bad.

I shifted off the wall and stepped forward. "Portia, we need to talk."

"We're going to talk, at lunchtime. Away from the office."

Her words were a sharp, crisp rejection; spoken in her slightly British—perfectly rounded and toned, I'm-up-here-and-you're-down-there—accent. Then she just walked past me, her body expressing her usual demeanor that said: stay away from me, you're worth nothing.

Shit. She was definitely regretting what had happened—awkward.

I went into the restroom but didn't use it, just stared at myself in the mirror over the basins. I wasn't that bad looking, was I? I ran my hand over my hair. I kept it buzzed short. I really didn't think I was that bad?

Bad enough to regret.

But then I wasn't rich and I wasn't Jason—white, Mr. handsome and nice from-out-of-town. Nope. I was straight out of the ghetto. Not Portia's type at all.

I was seriously surprised she'd gone anywhere near me if I was being honest with myself.

But dishonest… I wasn't that bad, and persistence and a bit of charm usually paid off.

I washed my hands and went back into the office.

Mr. Rees came in a few minutes later. That would lift the mood. The man was a tyrant and as arrogant and ignorant as Portia. Really, what the fuck had made me want to kiss her… Oh yeah, her in a bikini.

I started talking to Jason, about the party again—about everything other than me and Portia in the pool. But I'd lay hot odds she was sitting at her desk listening, fearing I'd throw in that little fact. Then all of a sudden Jason got up…

"Hey, I'm talking."

"I got something to do."

Well, I knew when I wasn't wanted. I was getting a lot of messages like that today. Lucky I had thick skin.

A few minutes later he came back with a look of thunder on his face and started shoving stuff in a box.

What was up with this day? "Where you going?"

"I just realized that this job's not for me. Bye..."

Nice fucking knowing you! I glanced over to see Mr. Rees watching Jason.

Well, what the hell was that about?

The girls were watching too. I could see Portia. She'd turned her chair to face Crystal and, having seen Mr. Rees, they were all pretending they hadn't been about to start gossiping, but any moment now, there was going to be a gossip fest...

Jason walked out without a "thanks", or, a "nice knowing you", or, "see you", or anything, and he looked pretty crazy with his cardboard box of stuff tucked under his arm, and an angry face.

I watched him go, feeling like my hangover from the other night had come back. Seriously, what the fuck was going on today?

And now it was nearly twelve-thirty.

Mr. Rees shut the door on his office. Normally I'd have gotten up and gone over to the girls—when the ogre had gone back in his cave—and they all began whispering. I didn't. I figured Portia wouldn't want me there. 'Course I could go over anyway, to wind her up, seeing as she was so embarrassed over having had a thing with me. But that was the sort of game my dad used to play; I wasn't that guy. If she regretted the stuff we'd done, that was fine. Let her regret. I didn't, and there were dozens more women out there to be fished and hooked.

When the clock in the left-hand corner of my screen rolled over to twelve-thirty, an email message flashed up. I opened it.

'See you there.'

Showdown time.

She got up, threw a red scarf around her neck and pulled on her coat, then threw her purse over her shoulder and walked out.

Here we go. I gave her a few minutes head-start so no one would think anything of me following, then got up too, and went to get my jacket. The shock of Jason going rattled through my nerves. The guy was there, then gone.

Mr. Rees came out of his office as I walked past, and I heard

13

him speak to Hilary, our sub-editor, asking for Jason's contact details to forward a letter of notice.

Jason had been sacked.

Shit. The guy had done nothing wrong. I'd better watch my ass. I was nowhere near as focused as Jason had been. Keith was always having a quiet word with me. Usually it was, "Don't talk so much," or, "You're too loud."

Shoving my hands deeper into the pockets of my jacket, I walked out.

When I reached Starbucks, a block away from the office, Portia was in the line.

I walked up and joined her.

"Hey."

She looked at me and turned red again. "Hey." She looked away, like she was looking at something else. Anything else—as long as she didn't have to look at me.

"You eating?"

She shook her head, her chin and her nose tilting up, like I was a bad smell, or something else disgusting.

The girl was not a great eater. She was always on the latest celeb diet. But she wasn't overweight.

Whatever, I decided to buy her a ginger muffin. I knew she liked ginger. For the last three weeks, the smell of her seasonal ginger latte had hung around the office when I'd walked into the office in the morning.

The guy looked over to take my order. She must have given hers already. "Black coffee, two ginger muffins, and one of those pepperoni things, heated."

The guy nodded at me and headed off to put it all on, to cut the line.

We moved along, not speaking.

When we got to the cash register, she reached for her purse...

"I'll get it." It was the manly thing to do, but when I took my wallet out, her fingers rested over my hand.

"No, it's okay, you don't have to."

"It's okay. I want to." My answer was probably sharper than it should've been, but I was starting to get a little pissed. I may have a millionth of the money her family did, but I could afford to buy her a coffee.

I really didn't think I was so bad. Maybe I was thick skinned—but I did have some pride.

She picked up her drink and left the rest for me to carry on a tray. She moved right to the back, probably to avoid anyone in the office seeing us together through the window.

Such a glowing assessment of my performance New Year's Eve. She obviously hadn't had as much fun as I had, although she'd seemed to be enjoying it at the time.

I slipped into the chair opposite her and lifted one of the muffins off the tray. "For you, eat it or don't eat it, whatever."

Her blue eyes, that were mid-gray in reality but reflected blue, glanced down at the plate and then up at me. She bit her lip then opened her mouth as if she was going to speak, her expression hardening. She shut it again, turning pink, saying nothing, and then gripped her cup with both hands and looked down.

The girl looked meek. When had I ever seen Portia look meek before? Never. Her arrogance was cringing. Her blush no doubt expressed the shame this preppy, society girl felt over slumming it with me.

"Portia, you asked me here to talk?" My pitch rang with sarcasm and impatience.

"Justin…" she said to her coffee, in a voice that told me off for my being cutting. It sounded a little more like the Portia I was used to.

"What?"

She looked up again and stared at me, appearing anxious. That was another new look for Portia, as far as I was concerned.

"I… we… did…?" She bit her lip, and then she came right out with it suddenly, "Did we do it? The other night… I mean… Shit…

Did we, you know? I was so drunk I don't remember."

So that was what all the blushes were about. I started laughing, I couldn't help it. Really I should be insulted; she looked so terrified, like it would be a scene from a horror movie if we had done it. "No. We didn't, Portia." The air swept out of her lungs and her breath brushed my cheek before she looked down at her coffee again.

I leaned back in the chair, trying hard *not* to feel insulted… "We kissed, and I made you come, and you never returned the favor."

That had her eyes and her color back up, along with her chin and her nose tilting. "Justin." It wasn't a shout, it was a hard whisper. "That would have been disgusting in a pool anyway."

"Nice to know you got your priorities right, Portia…"

She screwed her face up at me—she even looked pretty when she screwed her face up.

"I take it you regret it?"

"I don't remember it. Well, only in the form of a few patchy images. I can't remember getting dressed, or getting home. How did I get home?"

I hadn't realized she was that bad. "I helped you get dressed and you were unsteady on your feet but you weren't out of it. We came back on the subway, and I walked you to your door."

"You did?" Her gaze was boring into mine, like she was looking for a lie.

"Yeah, I did."

"Thank you." Those words were reluctantly said, and she looked away, but as she spoke she reached out and picked a piece off the muffin I'd bought her.

"You're welcome."

She glanced up again.

I picked up my muffin and took a bite, watching her as she watched me. So what now? Did I want this to be something, or was it just a hook up.

I didn't say anything, nor did she.

Then eventually, after she'd nibbled a couple more pieces of

16

her muffin, I said, "Do you regret it?"

One of the staff set down my toasted pastrami thing.

Portia took a breath as they walked away.

She did regret it.

"I—"

"Forget it, Portia. We hooked up at a party, it's nothing big, it probably happened a ton of times all over New York. Two people had too much to drink, end of, no headline."

Portia

End of. Justin was right. I was embarrassed, and I felt awkward as hell, 'cause I couldn't remember exactly what we'd done, but I believed we hadn't gone the whole way. I hadn't had any flashbacks of that, and as soon as he'd said he took me home, I saw an image of him next to me in a subway car.

"Sorry." Embarrassment led me to say it.

He shrugged. "So anyway; what the frick went down with Jason?" There was a sudden glint in his brown eyes.

Wicked and funny. That was Justin.

He always joined in with the gossip but we never knew if he was making fun of us when he did. Crystal's theory was that he was a douchebag and he was joining in with the hope of getting lucky. Well if that was true, his moves had worked on me. I was staying sober from now on. Resolution.

"What the hell you gonna do, Portia? You won't have pretty boy to stare at every day… Shame. You've got no chance of pulling him loose from his girl now…"

"I wasn't trying to."

He lifted his dark eyebrows. "Yeah, right. Whatever. You aren't fooling me. If he'd have offered, like I did…"

Crap, he had to go and bring that back up. My skin heated. I was tired of blushing. I'd spent yesterday with my head under the pillow, too embarrassed to even face myself. "Don't talk about it."

"Was I that bad?" He was joking but he wasn't joking. I'd kicked his ego in the balls.

I gave him a lopsided smile and narrowed my eyes, "Justin, I told you. I don't even remember!"

His eyebrows lifted higher. "Great. That bad." His wide lips tilted. He wasn't unattractive. I'd never really looked at him like that before. But he was okay. I mean his eyes were nice, dark brown and glowing like treacle, with that wicked and humorous glint, and he had a wide smile that came in flashes. His short black hair, that he kept cut close to his head, suited him because he had a nice shaped head… That sounded stupid. But he did. I wanted to reach out and touch him, run my fingers up his cheek and then over his hair. Maybe that was how things had got started in the pool.

He was talking about Jason again. I wasn't really listening.

"… so you girls are going to miss the eye candy."

I smiled at him, and just nodded. I wasn't going to lie. Jason was hot. I could just watch him for hours.

"We oughta get back." He stood. "Otherwise we'll be the next to be fired."

I got up.

When we reached the office, he held the door open for me. Crystal was wrong. He wasn't a sleaze. He was just a normal guy—girl hunting. He was nice in a way. He'd made this whole thing with me easier. He could have been really horrible.

He whispered in my ear, "We better go back separately, seeing as we're incognito… You can go up first, I'll hang back."

I smiled at him, "Thanks," then walked on ahead.

I glanced up when he walked into the office five minutes after me, and watched him take his black Parka coat off on the other side of the room. His body wasn't that bad either, I remembered. He had abs. He'd looked pretty good in the pool.

Another blush raced over my skin and I looked down at my screen before he caught me watching. But ten minutes after he'd sat down I sent him an email, giving him my cell number, with a message saying… "Why don't we be friends outside of work? If you want? What's your number?"

A second later an email came back from him. It was just his number and nothing more.

I looked up and leaned 'round my screen to see him, but he wasn't looking at me. He was staring at his screen, like he was totally focused on work.

Justin

"Justin!" My kid brother, Dillon, hurtled out the school gate, right into my belly, with his backpack falling off his shoulder and smacking me in the thigh.

"Hey Dillon, woah. What's up with you, kid?"

Having hugged me, he pulled away, laughing. "Nothin'." His eyes were shining with a I-love-my-big-brother look of idolization. That look got me in the chest every time, with a sharp bite of affection.

"Did you have a good day?"

"Yeah." He liked school but he hated the after club he had to go to when Mom was working and I had to pick him up.

"Dillon!" A pretty little girl with braids shouted over, taking her mom's hand. She did a huge exaggerated wave, the way young kids did.

My already super cool and chilled little brother just lifted his hand. "Bye Miah."

I laughed. He looked up at me, taking my hand. "Are you working on the ladies already little bro?"

He laughed. Then he said, "She does like me but it's annoying. She hangs around all the time when I just wanna play."

I gripped his hot, sticky hand tighter, looking up the street watching the traffic and getting ready to cross. "Well, one day, you are gonna be begging girls to just hang out with you."

He made a disgusted sound, and I glanced down laughing at him. "Urrgh, no way. I don't wanna play with girls..."

For now. The day will come Dillon when you will love playing with girls... I didn't say that. Just smiled at him, wishing I'd had

19

a childhood like he did.

He may have to go into after-school club but he never had to comfort Mom like I did at his age, after her and Dad had fought, and he'd knocked her about, or after he'd had a run in with the cops and ended up in jail.

When we'd crossed the street, Dillon let go of my hand and started telling me about his day. Telling me all the eight-year-old-kid gossip from his school. I loved it when he did. He made me laugh the way he talked with a blazing fire of excitement, at a hundred miles an hour, and the flames of the excitment in his belly flickered over his facial expressions and in his eyes too.

Along the street I saw Jake, waiting on the corner of the side-walk, where he always met us. He turned the corner and walked on as soon as he knew I'd seen him.

Met us—was a loose term. He never actually bothered waiting for us, or spoke to us, but walked two hundred yards ahead of us, pretending he didn't have to walk back home with his fricking annoying older brother and the baby of the family.

Dillon chatted on. He didn't care… Jake only stirred me up, no one else… and he knew it.

How the fuck had I ended up being treated like our frickin' shit Dad? I didn't know. But Jake treated me like I was his parent and not his big brother. He had an inbuilt button that said—do everything the opposite of what I said.

My cell buzzed, vibrating in my back pocket. I pulled it out. A message from Portia. Dillon kept talking.

It was a stupid picture of some weird dressed-up dog in a park. I laughed. Then another text came in.

'Thought I would send you that to make you laugh. Did it?'

'Yeah, it did.'

She could have punched me when she sent me her number. I hadn't expected that, and I'd played it cool, just sending her my number back. But now she'd sent the first text too. What did that say?

The girl had my attention whether she wanted it or not.

"What did you laugh at?" Dillon's brain finally caught up and overtook his mouth…

"Here." I showed him the picture of the Jack Russell dog wearing a red and white wooly hat, sweater and scarf… He laughed too.

I slipped my phone back into my pocket, then rubbed a palm over Dillon's hair as he started up with his eight-year-old bullshit again.

Jake was at the end of the block and about to turn, heading for home. I wished he'd wait. Our neighborhood was one of the worst in New York; kids 'round here always claimed they didn't have a choice about being in a gang. Gangs were what people did. But not me. I'd stayed in school, kept my head down, paid my way through College, working in a Mackie D's, and now I was doing my best to keep my brothers out of all that shit.

My heart thumped steadily like it did every day when we walked back and Jake disappeared out of sight. Dillon kept talking, and I commented, laughed, and said all the things I was supposed to in reply, but my mind was on Jake.

There were loads of drive-by shootings in our neighborhood. Stabbings. Fights. For no better reason than people just wanted to show they were frickin' tough. That wasn't tough, that was cowardice. Tough was fighting against a life, and hood, that tried to hold you back.

My mom was tough. She'd escaped one of those guys. A guy who used to bring all sorts of crap back to our door and beat her up—and he'd slept around.

In a hood like this, she was bringing up four boys alone—working her ass off to do it.

Dad had thought himself tough. He'd grown up in a gang. He'd ended up leading it. But Mom *was* the tough one.

Maybe sometimes it made her seem like she didn't care but she cared her heart out about us. Dad had just beaten all the softness out of her. Our mom cared with venom. She fought fiercely to do the best for us.

Respect.

I loved her.

We got as far as the street corner Jake had turned. When we turned it, there were a few kids in a car near him. My heart played an erratic base-beat against my ribs.

I settled a hand on Dillon's shoulder, and drew him close against my hip as we walked on. He kept talking, oblivious to the tension that rattled about inside me. My eyes were on Jake. He kept moving, but the car slowed down near him. Shit. Come on... I was too far away to do anything. If the barrel of a gun appeared out the car window, Jake was a corpse, there was no way I could cover the two-hundred yards between us and do a single thing to stop him getting wiped out.

The car crawled along beside Jake, and a kid in the back seat wound down the window. I was walking faster without even thinking about it.

Dillon started half-running to keep up. "What is it?", he said as he looked up at me, sensing my tension and realizing I hadn't heard a word he'd said for five minutes.

I glanced down at him. "Nothing." I kept my hand on his shoulder, so he couldn't run off and get anywhere near the car.

Something was said to Jake, but as far as I could tell, he didn't answer, just ignored them and kept walking. Good boy.

The car pulled away speeding up, and then the wheels screeched as the back window got wound up, and it accelerated away up the street.

This was our walk to and from school. It was like stepping through a field of landmines. We regularly past burned out cars some kids had crashed joy riding the night before, then torched. As well as kids standing on street corners with their hands inside their jackets or their jeans, like they had a knife to flick at you any moment... They just wanted us to be scared.

I wasn't scared for me. I was beyond the reach of gangs. I had my education. I had my job. And I had a decent life. And, yeah, I stood out in this neighborhood like a beacon, 'cause going to college had made me speak different and act different, but I kept my head down and my nose out of the gangs business and they left me alone.

But my brothers... It was my brothers I worried over.

Jake's movement was a little stiffer and his stride a little longer. He was trying not to give away a single sign he had been rattled by whoever had been in that car, but he had been rattled.

I'd tell Robin and get Robin to ask him what was said. If I asked Jake, he wouldn't answer. But then if I told Robin Jake would know the question had come from me anyway... Maybe I just had to leave it and trust him. He'd probably been just as scared as I was that the barrel of a gun was gonna come out of that rolled down window.

Chapter Three

Portia

When Justin walked into the office my gaze got stuck on him. I had been looking at the door waiting for him to walk through it. I smiled, my cheeks heating as he caught my gaze and smiled too.

When he smiled he was actually pretty good-looking. I liked his smile. I liked his relaxed way of moving too. Justin was the antidote to me. He was soooo laid back he was horizontal, and he had New York swagger. Justin was the polar opposite of my last boyfriend Daniel. Daniel had been rich, upper-class and up-himself.

I realized I hadn't looked away. I'd been staring at Justin, watching him walk along the office, probably with a dumb besotted look on my face. The more I looked at him, the more I liked the look of him, and of course in my subconscious, memories of a certain New Year's Eve night in a pool still hovered. My opinions about Justin were shifting at a rapid pace.

When he got nearer, I turned to look at my screen, that was still a spinning wheel, with a message saying 'Welcome.'

His fingers touched my neck, they skimmed over my skin, a light slide of his fingertips along the inside of the collar of my blouse. I shivered, and the sensation ripped right through my middle to my belly, making me ache between the legs.

Heat burned my cheeks. I picked up my cell, feeling the need to say something to him. Anything…

'Did you have a good night?' I sent the text and heard his cell buzzing in his back pocket as he hung up his coat.

He didn't reply straight off, but he took his cell out just before he sat down, then smiled over at me, nodded a little and winked.

Shit. Even that stupid little gesture flipped my belly.

'I did. Did you spot any more dumb dressed up dogs in the park? I fancy something to laugh at.'

':-) Sorry, no.'

':-) No matter then, but if you think of anything to make me laugh…'

'I'll text you :D'

'Yeah.'

Why did it feel so good talking to him? I had this warm sensation in my belly.

Probably because I was sad—in the pathetic sense of the word—and I was heading toward becoming one of those old women with a cluttered house and a hundred cats. I was friendless and lonely. Yeah, I had Becky and Crystal at work, but we didn't get together much outside work. We were not BFFs, we were just girls who got on okay in the office. I didn't even know if they really liked me…

Whatever, I'd been on my own for a year, I could cope with being on my own.

'What are you thinking about?'

I looked up and saw Justin standing, diagonally to me, on the other side of our block of desks. He lifted his phone a little. Probably to tell me to answer.

I smiled, then looked down to text.

'My boring day in the office.'

':-) Cool as long as there is nothing wrong.'

'There's nothing wrong.'

The guy had a sweet streak. How come I had never seen that before? I'd watched him befriend the new starter, Jason, back in the summer, and while Becky, Crystal and I were on good terms, he and Jason had been really thick… Like always talking…

He went over to the kitchen, probably to get a coffee. I watched him again. I loved the way he walked. Was that a crazy thing? To like the way a guy walked…

Watching how he walked had the quivering feeling tickling in my belly too.

'Do you want a coffee?'

He texted me. I couldn't see him. He was in the kitchen.

'Yeah, thank you.'

'It'll be with you in a moment. Ma'am.'

'Fool.'

':D Just thought it might make you laugh.'

My lips lifted in a closed lip smile and a chuckle of amusement tickled in my throat. I really liked him now. How come that had happened?

Justin

I set Portia's coffee down on her desk. It was the fourth day I'd made her coffee. She looked up at me, giving me one of those tight-lipped smiles of hers that implied she still knew I was way beneath her on the social ladder but she was thinking about letting me climb up the rungs a little. I went back to the kitchen for Becky's and Crystal's coffee.

I had started making them all drinks, so it didn't stand out that I made Portia one. They thought it was my New Year's resolution; to suck up and make them coffee. 'Course they hadn't actually picked up on the fact that I always gave Portia hers first. 'Cause she was the hottest girl and the one I was chasing. Mildly. It was no big deal if our texting and coffee-making went nowhere at all—but equally, if it went somewhere… I'd welcome another New Year's Eve pool moment with her.

And she did keep texting me, only about stupid stuff, but she wasn't cutting me.

"Hey, did you see this?" I caught sight of Becky dropping a

magazine on Portia's desk, folded back, to show Portia something on a particular page.

When I came back with Becky and Crystal's coffees, all of them were clustered around Portia's desk, jawing in catty voices about some celebrity gossip in the magazine, cutting some poor famous woman down to shreds for having put on a few pounds, laughing at the before and after picks.

I don't know. I mean, I liked Portia, physically. She was seriously attractive. But her bit-of-a-British accent and her tipped-up-chin-and-nose, saying I'm-better-than-you-back-off, gave her a hard edge that was sharp. Maybe there was something there or maybe there wasn't. She was brittle really. She had a personality that was like stone. If she was really interested in me? Would I be interested in that?

She glanced up before I could turn away and caught me staring at her. There was a really tiny twitch at the edge of her lips. Then she looked back down.

Shit, that little twitch in her lips had a little twitch shifting in my dick. It ran up my nerves and lust gripped like a sudden punch that knocked the air out of me.

I guess I could overlook her similarity to stone. Maybe it would be fun to go up against such a hard edge in a bed anyway.

Portia

I caught Justin's eyes widening, and his lips tipped sideways just before he turned away. The smile that had involuntarily lifted the edge of my lips spread.

There was something going on.

I was sure he was making a play for me.

Every day he made me coffee, but he made it for Becky and Crystal too. Yet he always brought my cup over first, put it down, and then went back for theirs. He was up to something.

Becky said something and Crystal laughed. I laughed a little too, though I hadn't heard what she'd said; my eyes and my attention were on Justin, watching him as he walked around to his desk.

I loved the way he moved. I mean, he had this relaxed way of walking but as he walked, you could see the strength of his character coming through. It was the way he carried himself. Justin was confident—comfortable in his own skin. He wasn't afraid of being judged. He didn't seem to care what anyone thought of him. If someone didn't like him; I think he would just shrug it off. He wasn't interested in impressing anyone. He was just who he was. No complications.

The main editor walked over to talk to him. It gave me more time to watch as he stayed standing.

While he talked with Keith, Justin's hand came up and gripped the back of his neck. Something trembled low in my belly as I remembered those long fingers touching me.

I still liked the shape of his head, the curve of his jaw. I don't know. Justin was just perfectly proportioned; it was like he'd been airbrushed in real life.

Keith said something and Justin nodded, his hand falling. Then Justin turned as Keith walked away. Justin's gaze didn't lift, he didn't catch me watching. He was looking at his screen as he sat down, his lips parting to let out a short sigh as he sat.

That meant he was working on something complicated. I'd started really noticing the sound of his little sighs that drifted across the desk. It meant he was thinking, working something out in his head.

The thought of his broad lips parting to let out a sigh had my blood heating and sensation tingling in between my legs. Someone must have turned up the heater in the air-con, I wanted to strip.

"Hey. What do you think?" Becky hit my shoulder with the back of her hand. I didn't know what she was asking; I hadn't been listening to them.

"Girls!"

Keith saved me anyway. He'd seen we were just talking. Becky and Crystal immediately turned away.

I sat back down; my mind spinning with unvoiced questions I wouldn't admit to as my mind fixated on Justin's lips and his hands.

I don't remember fixating on anything about Daniel, my ex. Daniel had always just been Daniel. We'd known each other for years before we got together. Our parents were friends. They'd pushed us together.

At the time, I'd thought I wanted that.

I looked up, but I couldn't see Justin around my screen. I thought about the way he moved; his confidence, his simplicity. No secrets. No games. No disguises and false fronts.

God how refreshing was that.

Daniel had been too like my dad in personality. But then I hadn't known what Dad was really like at the time I'd started with Daniel. I'd been blind still. Seriously, it was as if I had never opened my eyes until the night everything had gone wrong.

How had I not known Dad was cheating; and how had I not seen how self-centered and pathetic Daniel was? I wasn't even sure he'd loved me at all. He'd loved himself, and he wanted to look good, and have the sort of influence my dad had. I was just part of that package. The girl who would look right on his arm. The girl whose inheritance would help fund the political career he was aiming for. The girl who knew how to act in that world… Except, I wasn't going to play any part in it. I hadn't even known everyone else was acting until my eyes had been ripped open.

I'd had to wake up and grow up quick. I'd cut my ties with my parents' wealth and their world and just walked away.

Dad hadn't cut me off. My trust fund money was still sitting in an account. Untouched. It felt like blood money. I didn't want it. I was making my own mark on the world. Doing what I wanted, not what they wanted. As far as I was concerned, I had no obligation to them. They'd lied to me, pretended they were something they were not. Just like Daniel.

Not like Justin.

There was another whisper of a sigh from the other side of the block of desks. I saw Justin's arm lift and his palm settled on top of his head as he stared at the screen, clearly trying to work out in his head how he was going to do something.

Justin was different from any guy in my world back home. The world that now seemed like a nightmare I'd dreamed up.

I'd arrived in New York alone; determined to do stuff my own way. I'd armored myself with the sort of confidence Justin had naturally. It had not come naturally to me. But I think I'd managed to convince everyone that I could do this—that I could make it by myself.

Yet beneath the person who'd conned everyone into believing I was thick-skinned, not-knockable and independent—was still that girl who had arrived in New York, alone and terrified of how she'd cope.

Justin was just Justin...

I was starting to really like him.

I looked down at my cell, my fingers itching.

I picked it up.

'Stop sighing, you're distracting me.'

I saw his hand fall from his head. Then there was a little amused grunt.

':-) I'm concentrating.'

'Well concentrate quietly :D'

'Ha. Ha.'

I had on the sort of smiley face I'd texted as I looked back at my own screen, and tried to get my brain to focus on work again, not on the guy across our block of desks.

Portia

I sat on the bed looking at Justin's number on my cell for about the twentieth time. I was so bored—and lonely. I was fed up of my own company Crystal and Becky weren't free and... and it was my birthday. Mum and Dad hadn't rung but then they were in Europe.

They were in Europe every winter, and always too busy to

remember the day they'd had me. But why did I care?

Because a part of me was still the child they had rejected for half my life, and then scarred irreparably when I'd discovered why.

My thumb hovered over the call icon again. Should I call him? What would I say if I did? I'd sent him a text first, after we'd swapped numbers, a picture of a stupid looking dressed up dog in the park that I'd seen as I walked home, just to break the ice. We'd sent a few texts since, all just conversational. It was a huge leap from that to calling and saying do you want to come over. But I needed some company.

I slid the call screen off my cell and selected messages, then typed: 'I'm bored.'

I sat waiting for five minutes, holding my cell in my palm, staring at the thing. It vibrated.

'Are you :-)'

Shit, what did I say? 'I want someone to talk to, and no one's free.'

'Are you hoping I'll be that person?'

I breathed out, not even realizing I'd been holding my breath. Anyone would do today. I just wanted some company. 'Maybe? I want someone to come over.'

'Portia. Are you asking me over or what?'

My stupid stomach did a somersault. Did I care that much if he came? No. It wasn't him. I just needed someone to spend my birthday with. 'If you want to come'… I didn't finish the sentence, I just sent it.

The reply came back immediately. 'If you're asking me'…

I didn't reply; my courage failed.

A moment later there was another text. 'Are you? Or aren't you?'

I took a breath. My fingers were actually shaking as I answered. 'I am. Will you? I'm lonely.'

'Ha.Ha. That, I do not believe.'

My hand was still shaking and I didn't know what to say.

At work they all thought I was a stuck-up bitch. I knew I sounded like that. I could hear myself… But… they didn't know

31

me.

My thumb lifted and hovered over the letters. I wanted to type, *please come*. But that sounded too needy. Sad and needy was the bit of me I hid from people. 'Are you coming over or not? I'm not asking again. Do you want to watch films here?'

'I'll come. Yes to films. I remember where you live. I'll be there in about an hour :D'

'Okay.' God, I couldn't believe how much lighter the pressure on my shoulders was, or how much my heart lifted, when it had no business giving a shit whether Justin came over or not. But I was twenty-two today. I deserved some company.

He arrived almost an hour dead from our last text, and even though I was expecting him, when the buzzer rang, telling me he was down at the front door. I jumped and then my stomach quivered with anxiety. God, this was madness. But it was Justin's company or no-one's, and no-one's was a far worse choice.

I had no idea where he'd come from—where he lived.

My fingers were stupidly shaking as I pressed the intercom. "Hi."

"It's Justin."

I pressed the button to free the door. "Come on up, I'm in the attic apartment."

Shit I didn't even know if he knew that. Maybe he knew that? Maybe I'd let him up here New Year's Eve.

My heart was going mad, I was so nervous—it pumped away with the pace of one of those crazy house music baselines like it was going to leap right out of my chest any moment.

I twisted the lock and went out. I'd rather be in control of this—*this time*.

On the landing, that was decorated in a modern eclectic style of peeling paint and mold, I leaned over the banister, looking down. "Justin!" He was on about the third flight of stairs. He stopped and looked up.

"Portia! What's up?"

I smiled. God, it felt so good to have someone here, I was

such a sad case. My fingers gripped the wooden rail as he looked away and started jogging up the stairs again. I'd worked with him for a year, I'd never considered him anything other than a work colleague before a few days ago, but now my eyes seemed to be seeing something else.

He didn't look any different though. His hair was cut dead short so he could hardly style it a new way, and he always had such a relaxed manner at work, he wasn't going to be suddenly more laid back. Justin was Justin. But I liked what I saw. I mean, he didn't have the obvious looks his friend Jason had had but he wasn't at all bad looking and as he rounded the corner of the flight of stairs that would bring him up to my landing, his brown gaze caught mine. The guy had really nice eyes, like light shining through a glass of cola. He was kind of close to a young Will Smith when he smiled and definitely Jason Derulo standards when he didn't.

I straightened up, smiling too. "Hey."

"Hey. So this is your space then?"

He hadn't been up here. That was good to know. "Yep. Come in." He was carrying some shopping. I turned and went back inside. He held the carrier out when he came in.

Justin

"This is for you." I held out the stuff I'd got in a store along the street, offering it to Portia. Arriving empty handed would have been lame. "There's M&Ms, vodka, cola and popcorn. All we need for a few hours of Netflix."

She looked uncertain but she took the carrier from my hand and checked inside it.

She was different outside the office. Her hair was down, and she was only wearing a sleeveless tee and a pair of skinny jeans that clung like a second skin. She looked like a different girl, a girl who might actually play a game of tonsil hockey in a pool with a guy about thirty steps below her on the social scale.

I knew she came from money but shit, you wouldn't know it

33

from the place she lived in.

She unpacked the stuff from the carrier and put it onto the tiny square of space she had beside a two plate burner.

I glanced about her room.

It was just a room, with a single bed, a few cupboards, the burner and a basin all-in. I'd researched her family in a bored moment when she started at the magazine and I knew her parents were loaded.

I didn't say anything as she tossed the packet of M&Ms and toffee popcorn on her bed. Then she looked up at me with those blue eyes that always seemed to judge people. "Thanks for coming over."

"You're welcome."

She made a face at me, a cute face, her nose wrinkling, I'd never seen her wrinkle her nose, or look cute, ever. Sexy? Always…

"Shall I put a film on now then?"

"If you want, unless you want to change plans and go out somewhere?"

"No, I'm happy to watch films, if you are? It's my favorite thing, getting lost in films."

When I'd got her text asking me over here, I'd been at the table with Mom and the others. We'd just finished lunch. Mom had seen my face. I think my expression had probably said: *What the fuck?*

"*I'm bored.*" What the hell had that meant? My mind had run through the fuck-buddy idea in my head. I mean, I'm young and I'm a guy. And after the party, there was reason to hope keeping her company might come with benefits.

Mom had fired questions at me as I'd left the apartment. But I was twenty-two. I didn't want to be entirely tied to her. There had to be some get-out time in my life.

"Why don't you sit down?" Portia asked, throwing a look over her shoulder at the bed as she turned away from me.

It was kind of intimate sitting on her bed. Maybe this seriously was a fuck-buddy thing, not just my wishful thinking.

34

I perched on the edge, my hands clasping together as my elbows rested on my parted thighs and I tried to keep a firm hold on my imagination—and my libido.

"You can take your coat off. You're staying aren't you?"

She was laughing at me internally; it was in the movement at the corner of her pretty pouting lips and it caught in the blue in her eyes and made it brighter. I smiled at her, giving her a look that told her not to tease me but I stood again to take off my jacket and hung it from a hook on the back of her door.

It must be weird, just having a bedroom to live in. It was about the same size as mine although I did share my room with Robin. But at least I had a living room to walk into and a couch to sit on. She just had a bed and on the other side of the room, a cupboard, counter and basin.

She poured the vodka into glasses and then added the cola and held one out for me to take before I sat down again. "Do you think it's too early for this?"

For a minute, I thought she meant me being 'round here when we'd only just started something, but then I realized she was referring to the drink… And besides, we hadn't really started anything. As I'd told her before—we'd just messed around in a pool at a party.

"At two? No way."

She put her drink on a chest beside the bed and picked up the laptop. I watched her face as she opened it.

She glanced at me. "What do you want to watch?"

Her eyes were definitely more blue than gray today. Maybe cause she had a blue sleeveless tee on. I shrugged. "You can have what you want. I'll even suffer the Notebook or the Break up; your call."

She smiled.

Beauty literally shone out of the girl when she smiled like that. I don't think I'd ever seen her smile that openly at work. She always looked sly when she smiled at work, like she was being coy when she was anything but.

"You're saved, I hate romantic stuff. What about a Final

Destination marathon, we'll start at number one."

I grinned at her. "You're on."

This was weird. I was sitting in Portia's room, by her invitation, talking about watching horror movies. Had I slipped into a parallel universe? She wasn't only thirty steps above me on the society ladder. She was about the same in looks—a whole mile out of my league. I'd pitch myself at eight, maybe scraping nine, but she was a full on ten.

She went back to concentrating on setting the film up. My gaze dropped to her chest, the tee she was wearing clung, tucking beneath her breasts. I remembered the feel of her breasts in my fingers. They'd looked pretty awesome in a bikini, the perfect fit for the heel of my palm to press them up, so my thumb could rub her nipple.

Beneath her tee, I could tell she wore a thin cotton bra. The shape of her nipples pushed through the layers of her clothing.

I shifted a little, moving out of her way so she could sit down, trying to distract my brain from the threat of a hard on. It definitely seemed, so far, that the undertone of '*I'm bored*' had not been a bootie call.

She put the laptop up on the side as the film started playing and sat down on the bed, slipped her shoes off and curled her legs up as she slid to the back of the bed, then leaned against the wall. Her body was illuminated by a beam of sunlight that suddenly pierced the cloudy day and shone down through the skylight above us.

The sunlight disappeared.

She reached forward for her glass.

I watched the opening scenes, feeling awkward again, like I didn't know where to put myself with her so close.

I didn't get why she was here though, I don't mean why she'd asked me, but why the rundown room? Her parents were rich.

I sipped my drink as she sipped hers.

"Err! This is so violent!" her nose screwed up. It had a perfect tilt to its tip. How could the girl look so sexy with her nose screwed up? She did.

"You picked it." My tone came out flat as I fought an urge to kiss her. It had been her who'd kissed me in the pool.

Her gaze spun to me, and a smile broke those perfect pink lips. She hadn't any make up on today.

"I don't dislike the violence and gore, it's just like OMG when it happens."

I smiled and shook my head at her, then threw the M&Ms over. "Open them."

Still smiling she did and took a handful for herself then passed them back to me. "You can take your boots off and sit on the bed properly with me…"

Shit, something lurched in my gut and gripped at my cock.

I leaned forward and unlaced my boots, then moved back on the bed with my knees bent up and my thighs parted while I rested my head against the wall. My forearm leaned on my bent knee as I still gripped my glass.

We watched the movie in silence eating M&Ms.

When actor number four met a vicious end, her cell started vibrating on the side by the laptop, ringing out *Counting Stars*. She picked it up and looked at the screen but didn't answer, her whole body hesitating as she took a breath. Then her thumb touched it to take the call.

"Hi, Dad."

"Thank you."

"Yes."

"I'm fine."

"Working."

"Yeah."

"Okay."

"Say, hi, to Mum."

"Yes."

"Goodbye."

Her pitch had changed when she was on the cell. It got more

arrogant, and British. Her dad was British. I knew that too.

She colored up a bit as she leaned over and put her cell back on the side, saying nothing.

God, I had to ask. "Portia, your parents are rich, right? Why the hell are you working at the magazine and living *here*?" My free arm thrust out to highlight the inadequacy of the shithole she was in.

She turned an even brighter red when she looked at me. Sirens blared on the film to mark another victim's death. Taken down.

"The money's my parents, not mine."

Well, yeah, but I'd have thought they'd have sorted her out somehow so she lived a little better than this. If I had money, I'd want to help my family. Our gazes held for a moment, but then she looked back at the film and her lip caught in her teeth for a second.

"You, okay?"

She nodded but she wasn't.

"What did he say?"

She turned back and smiled at me. "Happy Birthday."

I was moving forward without thinking, and I gripped her arm. "It's your birthday? Why didn't you say? I'd have got you something. No wonder you were bored alone. We should do something. Go out..."

"*I want to watch films.*" That pretty pout was back.

"I could have bought you cake."

"You didn't have to buy cake and you did get me something, you bought M&Ms, popcorn and vodka."

I ignored that. She was just changing the subject. "Are you seeing them?"

"No, they're in Switzerland."

"Really? Were they here for New Year?"

"No."

"You didn't see them the whole of the holidays?"

"Nope, nor Thanksgiving. I see them in the summer when they come over to LA."

"*In the summer?*"

She looked at me with a flat gaze that said, *so*. It wasn't abnormal for her.

If this was a rich kid's life, I was glad all those wishes I'd made on birthday candles as a boy hadn't come true. "What about when you were a girl?"

"I was in boarding school, I stayed there."

Her expression said she didn't care. But she'd grown up on her own. A frown crushed my brow—I'd got her wrong in the office. But now she did look like the girl I'd worked with for a year. Her lips had pouted and her chin was up, in that aggressive bitch like expression I knew well.

"How much did you see them?" My hand ran over my hair, back and forth, as I said it. I was still knee deep in shock.

"A few weeks every year."

A few weeks? Well that had probably been as much as I'd seen Dad when he was meant to be with us, but that was because he didn't give a shit and was in and out of jail—what about her parents then….

"That's crazy." The words slipped out of my mouth before I realized I'd said them aloud.

Her gaze burned into mine, and then there was the girl I'd met today, the one who looked uncertain as she bit her lip an instant before saying. "Not in my world."

She moved to pick up the popcorn and focused on pulling it open then sat back and started slipping the burst kernels into her mouth.

I smiled, pity probably leaking into my eyes. She didn't look like she'd had a happy childhood. Maybe that's why she was so arrogant—*self-defense*. Maybe that office expression of hers wasn't aggressive but defensive?

"Are you sure you don't want to go out and do something, we could go to a bar, or—"

Her gaze spun to me as sharp as a blade. "No I'm fine. I want to stay in."

Nope, she hadn't been happy. She looked away, and I shut up and let her watch the film. She had her knees bent up in front of her now.

"Do you want more vodka?"

She nodded, so I got up and topped up her glass, not adding anymore cola. Then I filled mine.

She didn't say anything as I sat down next to her again, just gripped her ankles and watched the film play out to its violent conclusion.

When it finished she looked at me for the first time since I'd topped up her drink. "Sorry, I'm shit company…"

I didn't know what to say. "Do you really want to watch these? You don't have to watch horror for my benefit."

Her shoulders shivered like a draft caught her. "Believe me, I'm not into rom-coms and happy endings; I like horror."

I always thought the two of us were entirely different but now… I felt sorry for her…

"Put the next film on. Then come over here…"

She didn't say anything as she downloaded the film. But once she'd got it going and slid back onto the bed, I lifted my arm and she did come over, slotting under it and leaning against me. Her fingers rested on my stomach. My abs gripped tight in a sharp spasm.

I liked her touching me. I'd liked her touching me in the pool. And it was nice having her tucked under my arm.

Portia was pear shaped, wider hipped with a tiny waist, and really slender on top. She felt delicate against me but it was kind of awkward. "Tell you what, why don't we top up our glasses and lie down and watch it?"

She threw me a suspicious smile but nodded anyway and straightened up. She fetched the bottle and brought it over to half-fill my glass, then she topped up hers before coming back with cola. "Neat or mixed?"

"Mixed." I let her fill my glass up and put it on the bedside table within reach. Then I laid down closer to the wall so she could fit on the bed in front of me.

I propped my head up on my palm as she tipped the rest of the M&Ms into a bowl. When she came over, she offered me some. I took a handful.

Then she set the M&Ms down and tossed the cushions from the other end of the bed, my way. "Use them."

I stuffed a couple beneath my head, with the sweet taste of M&Ms flooding my mouth.

She put her drink down next to mine, then lay in front of me, on her side, one palm tucked beneath her cheek as she carried on watching the film. I slipped my arm around her, my hand resting on her belly. Was it possible to call a girl's belly pretty. She had a pretty belly, tight, and the cotton of her sleeveless tee brushed over her skin, riding up a little.

Interest stirred my cock. I focused on the film instead of her body. She didn't want me prodding her in the back; the girl was in a down mood.

"What are your parents like?" She asked.

That question came out of nowhere. She was still looking at the laptop, watching the film. "Dad's gone—"

Her head turned so she could look up at me. "I'm sorry…"

"No need to be. Mom threw him out. He was a douche, we're better off without him."

"We?" Her blue eyes were still looking up at me.

"I've got three brothers. Robin's seventeen, Jake's fourteen, and Dillon, the baby, he's eight."

"That's a lot of brothers."

"That's a lot of trouble." I grinned at her. "I've got the task of keeping them in line."

Her gaze changed, like it was looking inward, not outward, and she turned to watch the film.

"Is your mum, nice? That must be hard work?"

41

"She's nice, though she's not above clipping us all around the ear once or twice and hounding me. But I respect her. She works, she keeps us all on track."

She nodded, still watching the film.

"What about your parents, are they nice?"

Her shoulder lifted in a shrug. "Yeah."

It didn't sound like they smothered her with love. Gripping her shoulder, I rolled her onto her back and looked down at her.

"They're okay, really, I'm just in a blue mood."

I took a breath as my gaze dropped to her perfect pink lips. I looked back up and met her gaze. "I want to kiss you, Portia, can I kiss you?"

Her answer was a nod. I leaned down, my fingers sliding to her side. I could feel muscle beneath the cotton of her top, as my tongue dipped into the heat of her mouth. I pulled back after a couple of brushes of my lips over hers and looked into her eyes—the blue was brighter, shinier. She hadn't just said, yes; she'd wanted me kiss to her.

I was winning a lottery today. Maybe all those birthday candle wishes were being answered after all. I leaned down and kissed her again, and her lips answered mine, brushing against mine. Then her tongue slipped out in search of mine.

After a little while, as her fingers ran over my hair, I slid mine behind her back and up under her top. As I kept kissing her, I popped the hooks on her bra free. She broke the kiss, her head pushing back into the pillows and her blue eyes looking up at me as my hand ran around, underneath her bra and her top, and touched her breast.

The air that left her lungs brushed my cheek as I leaned to kiss her jaw, then her neck. I remembered the texture of her, and her breast might be small but it was just right. Her nipple peaked, pressing into my palm.

I bent my head lower as she sighed and arched beneath me. Lifting her top I exposed her pale skin. She moaned as I caught

42

her nipple between my lips and tugged, then let go. The girl was beautiful.

I sucked on her nipple for a little while, as I'd done in the pool the other night and skimmed my fingertips across her skin. The muscles in her belly tightened.

Her fingers stayed on my shoulders and my head, while her body moved beneath me, arching and falling, asking me to move between her legs.

I ran my fingers over the silk soft skin of her belly to her jeans. The metal button was cold. I freed it, before undoing the short zipper. Her nipple slipped out of my mouth and I met her gaze as I slid my hand into her panties.

She smiled, before shutting her eyes and biting her lip.

She was wet and warm, and major temptation, and I was rock hard. I rubbed my fingers over her, answering the rock of her hips, and then pressed two fingers into her heat.

She sighed.

Her breath was hot on my cheek as I watched her expression. She was working it, moving to get the most out of my touch as my thumb brushed the most sensitive part of her.

This was how she'd come the other night, just like this.

I lowered my head to her breast. She was writhing in moments. When she came it was warm sticky liquid around my fingers and a pulling sensation inside her. She let out a long sigh, just as she'd done in the pool. That sound…

Shit, this girl had a way of crawling inside my soul. I wanted to be in her physically. But today wasn't the day.

I let my fingers slip out of her and rolled to my back, looking up at the skylight as she recovered.

My cock was pressing hard to escape my pants. I breathed in, trying to drop my heart rate from a manic dance beat to a melody.

She rolled to her side. Her top was still bunched up and her pants undone as she cradled her head in her palm and stared at me, giving me a closed lip smile, with sparkly blue eyes.

Yep, today, they were definitely blue.

I rolled to my side too, my erection finally starting to descend. "That was what you forgot the other night at Mr. Rees's party, that's what we did, Portia."

Her smile broke wider. "That was good, but don't you… want sex…"

I smiled. "Not today, you're tipsy and in a blue mood, you'd probably regret it tomorrow. Take it as a birthday present."

"Well, it was the best birthday present ever." Her smile widened. She'd lost all the reserve she had in the office. "Thank you," she breathed.

"Welcome. The movie's ended, are you sure you don't want to go out?"

She shook her head. "Would you put the next one on?"

I smiled at her. "Yes. Straighten yourself up, and I'll get you more popcorn."

We spent the next couple of hours cuddling and occasionally kissing, watching the other films.

I left her just after midnight, with a long kiss at the downstairs door.

On the way home, my heart was fucking racing to the beat of the music pounding through my earphones as I sat on the subway train. My life had hit a junction and somehow I'd slipped lanes. It was sending me down a new track. Guys like me didn't get lucky with girls like Portia. I hit my forehead with the heel of my palm.

What the fuck?

Portia fucking Hemming was into me.

How the frick did that happen?

Chapter Four

Justin

My cell buzzed, vibrating on the bedside chest. I was lying down, but not in bed, scanning the funnies on You Tube. I picked my cell up to see who'd texted. Portia.

'Can you come over? I need you.'

'Need me?'

'Yeah, as in yesterday afternoon relief.'

':D R U, coming!, babe'

'Yeah, but I want some company.'

Well this was the girl I did know, the one who'd been lusting after my friend Jason for months.

'Come over', she urged again. 'Will you?'

'Yeah, but it'll take me an hour.' I didn't mind being second-best if this was the prize.

'Don't give a shit, come, and be quick.'

I laughed. 'Coming, just putting my boots on.'

'Then stop texting and do it.'

':D'

':P'

I looked over at Robin, he was asleep.

"Justin?" Mom was in the living room, when I grabbed my jacket off the hook in the hall. She saw me through the door. "Where are you going? It's late, child."

She hated any of us going out, and late was worse. She imagined all sorts going on in the dark, but to be fair, in our neighborhood, everything she imagined probably did go on. "I'm not getting into trouble. I'm going over to a friend's."

She stood up, her hands fisting on her hips, as she stared me out. "At this hour?"

"Yeah, Mom. I'm twenty-two. I can do whatever."

"Honey…" Her hands slipped off her hips and she moved toward me, like she was urging me not to go.

I gave her a look. "I'll text you when I get there, okay? So you know I'm safe. And I'll keep my cell in my hand set up for an emergency call all the way there. But just so you know I'll probably stop out. I'll be back to walk Dillon to school." I didn't wait to hear her answer. I headed to the door and went out, pulling it shut behind me with a click, careful not to wake the others.

Portia's family were non-existent, mine were the opposite—suffocating.

I texted Mom when I got off the subway near Portia's. 'Here, safe, you can go to sleep now. See you tomorrow.' I switched my cell off then. I didn't want to read a barrage of texts asking who I was with. I wouldn't have answered anyway.

The subway had been quiet, and the streets were too; just a few drunk people about, on their way home from clubs, and a few homeless people curling up under blankets in the alleyways. That was a shit way to live, it was freezing tonight. I pulled the collar of my coat up, and got some suspicious looks off people.

Was walking alone after midnight that weird?

Only if you were black! If you were black, then you must be up to no good.

When I reached Portia's, I pressed the buzzer for her room and leaned closer to the intercom. "Hey."

"Hey," she answered. "Come up." The lock clicked. I pushed the door open, my heart pounding out another base beat. She was leaning over the bannister when I looked up. A tremor slid through my belly all the way down to the tip of my cock. Shit. She was in a sleeveless tee again, and she had no bra on, the cotton clung, and she wore loose pajama bottoms with it; they could be pulled down in a second.

Shit. I had a semi just looking at her.

Her loosely braided hair slid around on her shoulder as she lifted a hand to say hi. Her hair looked like it was just waiting for my fingers to unravel it.

She looked awesome—edible.

Portia

When I caught sight of Justin, something hungry and desperate spun like a coin in my belly, then rolled in a spiral to a sweet ache between my legs.

I'd been lonely, and thinking about yesterday, all day. Literally every moment there had been some image of him haunting me. But it was a good ghost, it had felt really nice having Justin around. He hadn't done anything sleazy. I was even gloating about when we'd kissed. He could have gone all the way and he hadn't.

Tonight I wanted to. I was so pissed off with being alone, and a heated need had been humming in my veins all day. The fire he'd started yesterday still smoldering.

When he got to the top of the stairs and stopped in front of me, smiling, I lifted my arms and rested them on his shoulders, pressing against him as I kissed him hard. Saying without words, *go on fuck me.*

He kissed me hard too, walking me backwards toward my door, like he wasn't even going to wait until we got on the bed. Inside he kicked the door shut with his heal and pressed me back against the counter where my kettle and stuff were, and his cold hand slipped under my top and cupped by breast kneading it; the heel of his palm pressing into me, as his thumb brushed back and forth over my nipple.

47

A ridge in his pants said my hunger was equaled by his.

In a moment, my top was over my head and gone. I unzipped his coat and he shrugged it off, but he didn't give me chance to get his top off, he was kissing me again, both his hands on my breasts. I flicked his buckle loose, unthreading his belt, then slipped two of his buttons free, and reached into his boxers, to stroke the column of hard flesh there.

The guy had qualities beyond his good looking abs and his kindness yesterday.

His fingers pulled loose the bow tying my pajama bottoms and then his thumbs slid them over my hips. They dropped to the floor in a whisper of material. A moment later his hands gripped my thighs, lifting me up.

I held his neck.

His dark eyes glinted in the moonlight pouring through the skylight into my room, shining with heat and hunger. He'd come all the way over here for this. He'd come because I'd asked him.

I pushed his pants off his hips. My fingers were shaking.

He was still dressed, but I didn't care, there was something sexy about him being dressed and me naked, and I loved the urgency. An ache caught in my belly as he kissed me as if I was the last girl on earth.

"You got a condom?" His voice was husky and breathless.

"Yeah in the drawer, there." I liked it that he hadn't come prepared. He couldn't have many one night stands.

He came back, gripping his pants with one hand, while he tore the condom open with his teeth. His gaze dropped to my parted thighs then lifted to my breasts, as I leaned back. When his gaze rose again, it caught on mine. He smiled. Even his smile sent shivers through me. It was a promise.

I watched him slide the condom on, anticipation sparking through my nerves.

Then he looked up, gripped the back of my thighs, pulled them wider, and pressed in. Oh shit.

He kissed me and it was beautiful. He set a tantalizing rhythm. It felt like being on drugs the way he determinedly distracted my senses. I was high. I slid my hands down his back and pulled his sweatshirt and T-shirt up.

He answered my silent request, stopped kissing me, and smiled as he lifted his arms.

I stripped his top half.

His body was… Wow… Etched in moonlight from the skylight, he was from some mythical world, not brawny, but beautiful—and chiseled out.

I laid my fingers on his pectoral muscles. They were tight, and the skin over the ridges and hollows of his abdomen was smooth beneath my fingers, as his muscles moved when he pushed into me and pulled out. He was intoxicating.

His fingers pulled on my thighs urging me to rock against him, as he looked down, watching the moonlight catch the movement between us.

I was going to die any moment if he continued this.

Then he looked up, his eyes shining, his gaze reaching into me a moment before he leaned forward and kissed me again. His tongue plunged into my mouth, as he shoved in between my legs.

That was it. I tumbled, free-falling into an orgasm.

I couldn't kiss him back as it spun out into my nerves, unraveling and reaching right down to the soles of my feet, pulsing in my palms too. Frick. That was the best orgasm I'd ever had. The guy knew how to do sex.

His fingers gripped the sensitive skin at the back of my knees and he pulled my legs wider still, then started moving more quickly. I hung on, boneless from my orgasm. Ripples of a new one trembled through my nerves, bubbling up to boiling point.

I bit my lip and caught his gaze. He stared into my eyes, driving me insane.

I was hot and sweaty, and… and… "Oh my God, Justin."

I came again, and the delicious ache spilled through me, in all directions, liquid gold.

Then he came too, and there was a growl of breath by my ear as his fingers clasped my knees much tighter and his head pressed against mine. My hands slipped to his slender buttocks. Yep, his ass was great too. The guy was a clear ten, naked.

He straightened up and withdrew. I smiled; probably a stupid Cheshire cat smile.

He looked down. "What the fuck. Bullshit. The condom's split."

"OMG." I turned and grabbed a tissue off the counter. "Use that. I'll get a morning after pill tomorrow."

He slipped the wreckage off and walked over to the bin, holding his pants up with his other hand.

"Sorry," I said, quietly, "It was old… and… regular-sized…"

He glanced over his shoulder as he flipped the bin open with his foot, and gave me a quick smile. "I'll take that as compliment."

"The size thing was meant as one."

He laughed.

I smiled.

Once he'd dumped the condom, he turned, his hand still gripping his pants. "Are you worried? I know I'm clean, you don't need to panic. I haven't got anything. I got tested after I found out the last girl I went with slept around a lot. I've been off it for weeks since that."

My smile twisted. "I've been off it for a year…"

His eyebrows lifted. "A year?"

"Since I came to New York."

"No way. I thought you had loads of guys dangling from leashes you kept on every finger." He was back beside me. I slapped his arm. He just smiled. "Well you're beautiful, Portia, and you were chasing after Jason, and eyeing up Mr. Rees…"

"I do not eye up Mr. Rees."

"Don't tell me you haven't been busy calculating possibilities…"

"Not like you think."

"Well anyway…" Justin slipped between my legs again, "I don't

50

want to talk about anyone else, or work, when I've got you naked."

"Are you worried about me?" I offered. He'd given me his history.

"Should I be?"

"No, I've only had one boyfriend. We were together for three years. We split up before I came to New York. He was my first, and I was his, so, you're safe."

His free hand lifted and his fingers brushed back my hair. "Sorry."

"For what?"

"I got you all wrong. I've been judging you by your preppy voice. That isn't who you are. That's just what you sound like."

I smiled.

"Who broke up with who?" he asked.

"I ended it, I wanted more. I didn't want to be my mum. Mrs Perfect, with a perfect house and a perfect life. I'm not like my parents. I'd have been bored... And he was so convinced I should think him perfect. He's from their world. His family are members of Dad's club in California."

"His club?"

"He doesn't own it. It's like a golf and sports club, where people like my parents hang out."

His brow furrowed. "Are you really not like them? Have I been judging you by your parents' money too?"

His words cut. That was an insult. I pointed at the room and then looked back at him. "Do I look like I am?" Irritation bristled in my nerves, cold anger as old conversations with my ex and my parents flew through my head.

He smiled.

I made a face at him. "I was brought up to speak well, it doesn't mean I treat the world like a playground, and other people like toys..."

"I wasn't accusing you, just saying... It's just, at work, you're different. And sorry, Portia, but you do come across arrogant, a little, and untouchable—a lot." Both his hands came up and gripped my head, his palms pressing against my cheeks as he looked into my eyes. "But it's probably because you've been on your own too long. I get you now—and you're not like that."

Anger still hummed in my head anyway.

He kissed me, brushing his lips over mine, again and again, sending my temperature soaring and my temper out the door.

My fingers gripped his hard buttocks and a sharp, nice, pain caught in my belly.

His fingers slipped under my thighs as he broke the kiss and whispered, "Why don't we get our money's worth out of that morning-after pill?"

That twisted an even sharper spasm in my belly.

He picked me up and my legs gripped about his waist as my arms clung around his neck. He turned and carried me to the bed.

I should be annoyed with him still, for calling me arrogant, but with his skin brushing against mine, and a prominent promise pressing between us, why the hell be angry?

He dropped me, kneeling over me, and I bounced onto the mattress, laughing. Then he straightened up and stripped off his pants, boots and socks.

The muscle in his legs and buttocks shifted under his glistening skin as the moonlight from the skylight painted him, and when he turned, his erection bounced, several inches of flesh pointing at me as he came down onto the bed…

Chapter Five

Portia

When Justin walked into the office, his hands were buried in the pockets of his Parka coat. He glanced at me, and as he did, he threw me a smile. I smiled too. He'd left my room at five a.m., after we'd had a second round, and then I'd fallen asleep for a little while.

He'd gone home to take his brother to school, so his mum could go to work.

A few minutes after he'd sat down at his desk I got an email. 'Did you get your pill?'

':-) Yeah.'

'Everything okay?"

'Yeah.'

'Do you fancy going somewhere for lunch?'

'That would be nice. But not Starbucks, the deli down the street.'

'Okay.'

'Come to my office.' Mr. Rees usually rang me, not emailed.

'Coming now, Mr. Rees.'

'I've got to go and see Mr. Rees, Justin. We'll catch up at lunch.'

'Yeah. Good luck!'

I grabbed my pad and pen, and headed over, instantly feeling like I'd done wrong. Every time I had to face him, I felt like that. It reminded me of having to speak to Dad when I was a kid. There was always something I'd not done well enough, and never any gratitude or congratulations.

The black eye Mr. Rees had come into work with the weekend after New Year had come down from a dark purple to a disgusting black and yellow. Someone had hit him, but he'd brushed it off and said he'd walked into a door.

Yeah, the sort of door with a fist on it. He'd pissed someone off.

"There's some letters on there." He slid the Dictaphone across the desk toward me. "I need them typed up today."

"Okay. Is there anything else, Mr. Rees?"

"And I need a present for my wife."

Why, what have you done? The gifts Dad bought Mum had always meant an apology. Maybe the guy who'd given him a pounding the other week was someone to do with the woman he'd been having an affair with, or his betrayed wife. I wished someone would deliver a similar judgment on my dad. He deserved it.

Yeah, Mr. Rees was like my dad—but a small-time version of him.

Dad had more money, more power, more reach, and probably more women…

"What type of present?"

"Something more than flowers, but it can go with flowers."

"Jewelry?" I thought of all the jewelry we'd discovered in a room we'd gone through back at his place New Year's Eve, his mistress's stuff. Maybe his wife had finally had enough and called him out…

I wished Mom would do the same to Dad… But she just ignored everything.

The day I'd caught my dad out, I'd had a massive argument with Daniel, and that had been the end of us, because he'd wanted me to agree that Mom's way was right. It wasn't.

"A necklace might be nice. I'm taking her out. She'll be wearing dark blue, if you can find something appropriate?"

I wanted to chuck his Dictaphone at him, call him all the crappy names he was, and storm out. I didn't, I needed this job, it was paying my bills, 'cause there was no way I was letting Dad pay them. I was done with being manipulated in the way people like Mr. Rees and Dad manipulated people—with money and presents.

Being reminded of that life dunked me in a bath of ice. It woke me up. Yeah he was like Dad, and his marriage was probably just like my parents'. Dad didn't have a mistress, as far as I knew, but he'd been with lots of other women, while Mum turned her back and carried on.

Romance. Happy endings. Love. Bullshit crafted by fairytales and Disney. I didn't believe in it. It wasn't what I was looking for. I'd made my mind up a year ago.

When I went back to my desk, I plugged in my earphones and listened to his dictation, my fingers moving over the keys automatically, as my brain skimmed through why I hated love.

I could still see Dad's face when Daniel and I had walked in on him dining with some twenty-something Swedish girl. He'd taken her out to a restaurant in a hotel twenty minutes from where we were staying, and left Mum back at our chalet. Shame for him it just happened to be the same restaurant Dan had decided to take me to. Or perhaps no shame—he didn't care—just asked me to say nothing so it wouldn't hurt Mum.

Dan and I went straight back to the chalet, and I saw from Mum's face, she knew what was going on.

When I'd been a child coming home on those rare occasions in the holidays, I'd watched him, always making people laugh. He was a social junky. He loved being around people and getting all the attention. But I hadn't realized then he'd been flirting too, and then I'd finally understood why he didn't want me there. His kid had cramped his style. That was why I'd been packed off to a British boarding school, so Mum could keep her perfect fake life and he could play away.

That was when Dan and I had split up too, because he'd agreed I shouldn't tell Mum, he'd said she was fine, she had what she wanted, a nice house and stuff… I'd told him to get lost. He'd flown back to California that night.

What I'd thought would be my own Disney tale of love with a happy ending had turned into a horror story. But it had opened my eyes. I knew the truth now. I wasn't writing anymore fairytales.

Justin

Portia hadn't looked at me all morning. She'd been staring at her screen, working.

I knew 'cause I'd spent half my morning glancing at her, all I could see was the curve of her cheek and the tip of her mascara coated eyelashes. Both times I'd seen her at the weekend she'd had no makeup on.

The Portia here wore makeup like a warrior; she was tougher.

I couldn't believe I knew the person under that. They were too different people. I'd got her completely wrong.

An email appeared in my inbox at ten to twelve.

'When are we going to lunch?'

'Whenever you want to go.'

'Twelve would be good, I've got to go out and do something for Mr. Rees after lunch.'

'Twelve then. I'll leave first and meet you there.'

Half an hour later we sat in the café, eating, facing each other. She was still her office self. She'd hardly spoken, just picking at her salad.

"I can't go out tonight. I've got to mind my brothers but tomorrow, Mom's not working, we could go to see a film if you want?"

"Is that a date?" Her pitch was sarcastic, preppy and cutting.

Shit, when she was in this mood, she could be a bitch. She was totally stuck-up, patronizing and superior today.

I frowned at her. "You know I said you were arrogant in the office. Well you're being arrogant. Yes, a date. What's so wrong with me asking you to go somewhere? Most girls would love that I'm asking you out and not just expecting sex."

She shrugged and took a mouthful of salad, chewing it at the same time as she made a face at me.

"So, do you want to go out with me or not? 'Cause I am quite happy with not going if you're going to get all stiff again—like I'm not good enough for you. Believe me, there are plenty of girls who think I am, Portia."

She swallowed her mouthful. "I didn't say that—"

"No, but you're acting like it."

She shrugged again and then blew out a long breath. "Look, Mr. Rees, pissed me off."

"Why?"

"Because he's like my dad. He wants me to buy his wife presents to smooth over some fight they've had. What's the value in me buying them anyway? It's meant to be him saying sorry…"

I leaned back in my chair, there was an undercurrent flowing.

She looked down at her bowl of salad, looking more like the Portia of the weekend, then left her fork resting on the edge of it and looked up. "I caught Dad out. He was with a woman. Mum just overlooks the affairs. Daniel and I split up over it, because he thought it wasn't an issue. I'm just not in the mood for a cozy chat."

I leaned forward again, and gripped her fingers before she could pull them back. "Believe me, Portia, I know what that's like. Dad played away the whole time my parents were together. Mom was always wondering where he was… and who with. I'm never gonna be like that. It's something I could never do. I've seen what it's like at the other end…"

Her fingers slipped from mine sharply. "I wasn't thinking of you. That isn't what we've got going on anyway. I'm just pissed off with Mr. Rees."

"You didn't seem to care at his party?"

"I was drunk at his party. I make stupid errors when I'm drunk."

"Including me?"

"Justin, stop putting words into my mouth—I'm pissed off with Mr. Rees, no one else. And yeah, I'll go to the cinema with you tomorrow night, but right now, I need to go and find his wife a fucking necklace. Perhaps I'll have it engraved, *P.S. your husband is a cheating bastard.*"

She stood up, grabbing her coat off the back of her chair.

"He has kids, Portia."

"I know. I wouldn't really do that. I'm just angry. Shall we do lunch again tomorrow?"

"If you want? If you're not gonna bowl into here like a tornado, and whirl off again…"

She shook her head at me. At last, I caught a slight smile.

I stood up too, and before she could turn and walk off, I grabbed her arm, turned her back a little and bent and pressed a sharp kiss on her forehead. It was like pressing an iron brand on her. I wanted this girl. I wanted her to be mine. Pride punched me in the gut when I'd first seen her today.

She gave me a shaky smile, then turned, her arm slipping from my grip.

Chapter Six

Portia

Oh my God, it was freezing, and I was starting to think Justin was a little bit mad. We'd been seeing each other for four weeks off and on, more on than off. At least twice a week he planned some outing, *a date*, and at least three times a week he ended up around mine and we had sex.

I'd bought a new pack of condoms, and we were nearly through it.

Today, though, today, the outing he'd planned was a picnic in Central Park. It would be really cool—in the summer—it was winter—and it was freezing. The grass had been white with frost earlier. Now the ground was just cold and hard, but he'd actually laid a blanket out on it, and he'd bought hot pastries from a deli round the corner, and hot chocolates. The guy was crazy. He had a wicked sense of humor, and he'd taken to teasing me constantly. He said it was to drag me out of my in-office moods.

Once, he'd stuck a post-it on my forehead at work when he'd walked past to go to the kitchen. It said: *out of office tonight*. We'd had a date planned, a trip to the ice rink and then to get some fried chicken.

Fortunately, 'cause he was always messing around, no one thought it odd, or guessed there was anything in it. They hadn't seen what he'd written. I'd screwed it up and thrown it in the bin.

I lay back, and felt the cold creep through my coat. I had three layers on—but I was so cold. It penetrated my gloves and hat. I looked up at the sky. It was clear blue and bright, framing the branches of a tree above us.

Justin was lying on his back beside me. He laughed to himself.

"What's funny?" I rolled onto my side and looked down at him.

I guess if I had to say who he most looked like, it would definitely be Jason Derulo, but Justin got better looking the more he smiled. He had charm and I was falling for it.

His brown eyes stared up at me, glowing warm like dark amber. "Just this. Just us. Just you. I still can't believe I've got a thing going with the office ice-queen. The climate suits you."

My palm hit his shoulder. "I'm out-of-office."

He caught my wrist and pulled me on top of him. I squealed, until his fingers gripped the back of my head and then he kissed me, slipping his tongue between my lips and holding my mouth to his. It was all that mattered in the world. Yeah, Justin had charm.

When he let me go, my palm rested on his chest and I looked down at him.

All around us other people were enjoying the park on a Saturday afternoon; kids ran about, a group of guys played a ball game, loads of people were walking dogs.

For a moment we stared at each other, then he whispered in a low voice. "Do you wanna go back to yours?"

"Yes." I did. We folded the blanket up and dumped our rubbish in a bin, then caught the subway train, fingers laced.

I had a sudden flash of fear. I kept getting them. A feeling that I was getting in too deep, too fast. But then I'd tell myself, I'm living for now, this isn't about tomorrow, or happy endings, it's about being happy today—and I was happy. Probably for the first time in a year. Probably for the first time in years—maybe ever.

When we got into my apartment he dropped the blanket on the bed and pulled my woolly hat off, then tossed that there too,

60

before kissing me, his palm at the back of my head.

There was no hiding from Justin. He said things like they were and he did things like they were.

When he broke the kiss he was unbuttoning my coat and I slid down his zip. Then we were peeling clothes off and dropping them everywhere, rushing to get into bed. He flopped back on the bed, pulling me with him, but I escaped his hold and went down on him.

"Shit." His voice rasped into the cold air in my room, as his fingers clawed in my hair. "Yeah, right, like that…"

In the last four weeks, I'd learned to do stuff just like him—no holding back.

I used my tongue to tease the sensitive pink skin at his tip. But his patience dried, or maybe he was going to come and didn't want to, because he gripped my neck and pulled me up. "Get a condom," he breathed at me urgently.

I reached to the drawer in the chest beside the bed, pulled one out, tore it open and then rolled it down, sheathing him. As soon as it was on, he gripped my thighs and pulled me up, then plunged into me, with a wicked smile.

Having sex with Justin was like riding rapids; a little dangerous.

His fingertips pressed into my flesh gripping my thighs. He'd told me he liked my hips and thighs—and most of the time we did it, his hands were there. But wherever he touched me, he sent luscious spasms winding through me.

He nipped at my nipple when I leaned forward.

Smiling at him, I held still, letting him push up into me, his thighs and hips working between my legs.

I looked down and watched his abs moving. The guy was pure gorgeous naked.

That thought made me come. It unraveled, reeling out into my nerves, catching in every corner and rushing right to my fingertips.

He tipped me back on the bed, and pushed my legs open wider; the beautiful cut of his abs and pecs, gilded by the sunlight

61

coming from above. He pushed into me hard, fast and relentless. All I could do was grip his shoulders and hang on, and he made me come three more times, the orgasms piling in on top of one another like waves rolling over each other on to a beach.

Poor Daniel—he'd been way out of Justin's league.

The next time I came I shut my eyes, and let him push me off a cliff, but this time he jumped with me; growling like a caveman he pushed hard in and then pulled a little back and did it again, pulsing inside me. His heart pounded in his chest beneath my fingers.

When I opened my eyes, his skin glistened with sweat and his eyes glowed as he looked at me.

"That was good," he smiled.

"Searching for compliments?" He was still inside me, and it felt so right.

His fingers cupped my breast, then pinched my nipple gently. "Say it was good, or your luck's out." His touch became a delicate threat.

I smiled and said nothing.

He pinched and I squealed, laughing. "It was good! It was good!" Shutting my eyes, I bit my lip, to avoid the pain of his grip.

When he released the pressure, I opened my eyes. He was staring into me, not just looking at me.

A surge of emotion rushed through me that had nothing to do with sex. "It was more than good, it was awesome."

Whatever the surge of emotion in me was, I saw it reflected in his eyes. "*You*, are awesome, Portia."

I smiled.

"You're pretty awesome too."

He slipped out of me, then got off the bed to get rid of the condom. "Flattery don't count when it has to be won, babe."

"Babe?"

He turned back and looked at me. "What do you want me to call you then, *darling*?" He mimicked my voice when he said it, stripping the urban out of his accent. I didn't want him to talk like me.

"You can say, babe."

"Do you want a coffee?"

"Yeah."

He made it, naked, as I lay there watching the really high, rounded muscle in his buttocks, and the long lean length of his thighs. I loved the way his ass curved into his lower back, and the line of his spine, and… everything… I loved everything about his body, including the shape of his head, I smiled to myself

He turned and smiled at me—his smile sent odd sensations spinning around in my belly.

After he'd bought the coffee over, he got back into bed with me, and we snuggled up under the comforter as he held me and we watched old episodes of the *Big Bang Theory*.

My life felt good, for the first time ever.

Chapter Seven

Justin

I watched Portia. She was working on some more dictation from Mr. Rees.

It was six weeks since the weekend after New Year's—since Portia and I had started something up. They'd been pretty good weeks. Mom had even come 'round to the idea that this girl might actually be good for me. She'd stopped worrying when I stayed out.

But I hadn't shown her a picture. I didn't know how she'd take the fact that Portia was white. Stupid. But Mom was gonna have to step out of her comfort zone. She was a traditionalist, she liked things just so. Portia's background and her family's money, was gonna throw Mom off track when she found out I was dating a society girl. She'd be anxious about it causing trouble for me.

Anxiety was stitched into Mom's DNA—by Dad's failings—and there was no unpicking it. She worried, and I hated making her worry, but I also had to live my life.

Robin had filled me in on the fact she'd been asking him a whole stack of questions. But he didn't know Portia was white either.

I breathed out the breath I hadn't realized I was holding; Portia was going to have to meet them soon. I wanted our thing to shift up a level. I wanted her to be my girl—in all my life. I figured Portia wasn't gonna step it up. She'd given no indication she wanted anything to change. If anyone was taking this up a gear, it was gonna be me.

I just wanted to stop hiding what we had.

Portia stood up and walked over to the printer to collect the letters she'd printed off. Her head was down scanning them for errors as she walked back. Her blonde ponytail had caught on her shoulder and rested over her white blouse. She had her work poker-face on. You'd never guess the out-of-office girl, I knew, was there.

I sent her an email. 'In-office.'

She sat down, and glanced over once she'd seen it. She smiled.

My fingers typed. 'Are we meeting for lunch?'

'Yeah, if you want.'

'I want, baby.'

':-)'

She hated me calling her babe or baby, but somehow, it softened her a little more.

'See you at twelve in the deli.'

'Yeah.'

She stood up then, smiling at me, with the letters she'd printed gripped in her hand, and turned to take them into Mr. Rees.

A little more than an hour later I stood outside the deli waiting for her, my hands in my pockets. This was one of the things I wanted to change. I didn't see why we couldn't just walk out of work together. Why did it matter? But it mattered to her, because whenever I suggested the idea she backtracked a mile, and came up with a dozen excuses not to.

I saw her, further along the sidewalk, walking toward me. She had on a black pencil skirt, a short cream coat and black patent heels. I knew beneath her skirt her sheer black stockings were stay ups. A spasm of lust, to touch her soft skin above her stockings, gripped in my groin. I ignored it. I couldn't even see her until Wednesday night.

If she'd been in out-of-office mode when she reached me, I'd have got a kiss—in-office Portia gave me a nod.

My hand slipped about her waist as we turned to the door, and I whispered to her ear. "In-office, baby."

She glanced back and gave me a big fat pleased to see you out-of-office smile.

It played guitar strings in my heart. I had it bad for this girl. I wanted it up a gear and I was gonna persuade her today.

"You, okay?" I asked when we sat down.

"Yeah, you? Are you busy?"

"Yeah, I've got loads to do."

"What?" She drizzled a bit of olive oil on her salad.

"I'm doing a feature on The Giants, Keith wants me to change the color tones, and the backgrounds, and ensure we're showing them in their best light—"

"Why does stuff like that matter?"

"'Cause everyone and everything has to look perfect these days, and it's all gotta be wrapped up in a parcel with a perfect bow."

She looked up and met my gaze. "And then someone comes along and breaks the glass, then you realize nothing is perfect, perfect isn't out there…"

She was thinking of her dad.

I reached out and gripped her hand. "But then sometimes you discover things are better than you ever thought they could be…"

"Portia! Justin!"

She moved in an instant, pulling her hand from mine and standing up, as I turned in my chair to face Becky from the office.

"Becky!" Portia gave her a hug and an air kiss. Becky looked at me, her eyebrows lifting. I smiled. It seemed my talk with Portia was off. The cat was out the bag.

"What are you two doing?" The question wasn't only in her words, it was in her voice as she stared at me, asking questions with her eyes too, guessing.

"Oh," Portia's hand waved in the air as she glanced at me only for a second. She didn't look me in the eyes. "He was in here when I came in, do you want to sit with us."

Bullshit. I wanted to grab her arm and make her tell the truth as she moved to pull up a third chair, encouraging Becky to sit. I felt like she'd punched me.

What the fuck, Portia?

She spent the next ten minutes gossiping with Becky like I wasn't even here, full on *in-office*, and then she actually had the fucking neck to throw me a smile and ask. "Why are you being so quiet? You're not normally quiet." If she'd been a guy I'd have hit her. *The bitch.* But I played along, and nodded at them, watching her in a dream.

Clearly what I thought had happened over the last six weeks, hadn't happened.

After another ten minutes, I'd finished my lunch and I'd had enough. Fuck this. I stood up, dropping my napkin on the table. "Well, nice to *run into you.* I'll see you back at the office."

She looked up at me, her eyes full of shock. She knew I was angry. Hell, Becky probably knew I was angry, but I didn't give a shit. Let Portia carry on her little games, but she'd be playing them by herself.

I walked out of the deli, letting the door bang shut. The good thing I'd had going was over.

I stuffed my hands into my jacket pockets and curled them into fists as I walked along the street, dodging people and grumbling to myself. I looked up at the skyline of scrapers—riled. Fucking hell, Portia!

Shit. I was pissed off and super angry when I got back to the office.

Portia came back fifteen minutes later with Becky. I knew she was there. I didn't look up. I also knew she was looking at me. Well, she could keep looking, it wasn't gonna get her anywhere. I was done.

'You okay?' Her message came up with a little envelope.

'Nope. It's over.'

'Over?'

'I'm done with you, Portia. The end.'

'Why.'

'The fact you even need to ask that says it all. Don't bother trying to talk to me.'

'Justin?'

I didn't reply. I really was done.

But when I went to the restroom later she followed. She was there when I came out. Standing in the hall, restless, like she'd been after New Year's when she hadn't remembered what had happened. Maybe I should have recalled that and known her heart was never in it.

"What?" I said to her.

"What's wrong." Her fingers touched my arm. I shrugged them off.

"Nothing's fucking wrong. Nothing at all." I moved to walk past her but she moved in front of me, and this time both her hands gripped my arms.

"What... You changed like in a minute, Justin."

She was painting it as me in the wrong. I wasn't in the wrong. I gripped her upper arms and shook her a little, to shake some sense into her. "I'm not gonna be your dirty secret. We're together and everyone knows it, or we're not. Why the fuck did you lie to Becky like that?"

"I..." She didn't have an answer; 'cause there was no answer. "I'm sorry."

"That's okay, Portia, 'cause I'm done, thanks for breaking the glass."

I let her go and walked past her.

She didn't come back to her desk for about fifteen minutes. I didn't look at her when she did.

She was nothing to do with me anymore.

Chapter Eight

Portia

My bed was cold. I looked up at the skylight. The full moon shone a square of silver light on my pillow. I remembered watching Justin making love to me, shrouded in it.

I couldn't believe he'd ended it.

It had been a week and I still hadn't got over the way he'd just cut the cord binding us together. He wasn't speaking to me.

He never even looked at me at work, though he was more playful with Becky and Crystal, like he was trying to annoy me. Or maybe he'd always been that nice and it was only now I really knew him I saw what I'd been missing.

He never answered my texts either.

I'd tried calling his cell, he just cut me off. I'd left about three dozen messages before I gave up trying.

He wouldn't let me apologize.

I'd tried twice at work too, catching him on his own. But he still ignored me. I'd given up entirely now.

But it hurt.

And I knew I'd hurt him, but I hadn't meant to. I hadn't realized how much he wanted people to know. I mean, he'd talked about it, but I didn't know he was pissed off over it… Obviously he had been.

I rolled onto my side, pulled the comforter up to my chin, curling up and hugging my knees. I ached for him. I'd never ached for Daniel. And it was a literal ache, it was in my palms and fingers; the soles of my feet and my toes. My belly and chest felt bruised—and my heart… My heart felt as though it had been kicked.

Tears rolled onto my pillow like they'd done every night since the glass had broken between us—fairytale shattered into reality.

I was bored and lonely again—and empty. I missed him so much. But I wasn't going to beg him to forgive me.

I don't know when I fell asleep but I must have fallen asleep because when I woke up, it was daylight. I looked at my clock. It flashed seven a.m. I stretched and sadness hit me like a brick smashing into my head. Why wouldn't he speak to me? If he'd speak to me, maybe he'd forgive me. I'd just made a mistake, it wasn't so bad.

I got up, washed and dressed—dead inside, my heart heavy.

My cell rang, *Counting Stars.*

I longed to see Justin's name when I picked it up, but it was Dad's.

I tapped the accept icon. "Dad…"

"Portia. We're in town, honey, we thought we'd come to New York for a weekend shopping. Can we meet up?" Of course they hadn't come to see me. No. They'd come to shop, and I was simply conveniently here. Like any other associate.

My stomach tied in a knot. Seeing my parents was hell.

"Okay, when?" There was no enthusiasm in my voice.

"Tomorrow, Friday evening, at six."

Panic hit my chest with a punch. "Okay."

"I'll text you the address of our hotel."

"Okay."

"Goodbye."

"Goodbye."

They couldn't even be bothered to see me today—*tomorrow.*

They couldn't even be bothered to come out to me—*our hotel.* They'd been to my place once, and turned around and walked straight back out in five minutes.

Nothing changed.

Except—since New Year's—I'd had Justin and I'd been happy for a while.

Well that was over and this was reality. I'd got sucked into the Disney myth again, that was all, things weren't different—and happy endings were fiction.

I washed and dressed for work, scraped my hair back into a ponytail, then gave myself a condescending look in the mirror. "Queen of mess-up."

Anxiety rocked inside me like the ocean swelling as I caught the subway to work. I hated going in now, 'cause I hated Justin ignoring me—and now I had dinner with my parents to look forward to too. Awesome.

I climbed the stairs to the floor our offices were on, delaying facing him by avoiding the elevator. But it was inevitable. When I walked in he was leaning on Becky's desk talking to her.

People started saying, "Hi," to me. He glanced up, but when he saw it was me he looked back at Becky, grinning and saying something, before he walked away and sat down.

Becky looked over as I got close. "Hey. Do you want a coffee? I was just gonna make one?"

"Hi. Yes. Thanks. That would be cool."

I slipped my coat off and went to hang it up, trying to ignore Justin who was ignoring me.

It felt like I was back at boarding school. Sharing rooms with girls always meant you'd fallen out with someone.

Maybe that was why I had grown up so tough. I'd had to be tough. If you let things like this—like Justin—beneath your skin, then you were lost and miserable.

I took my seat, and made a decision to have one more try…

'I said I'm sorry, Justin.' I sent the email.

71

There was no response.

He was pretty tough-skinned too and obviously not miserable. But then he had his family, he didn't need me.

I needed him.

Sighing, I got up to collect Mr. Rees's mail. When I sorted it there was a solicitor's letter in there from a firm in Oregon, about a paternity case. That rocketed up my anger. Was that the reason he'd been black and blue and buying his wife presents a few weeks back…?

It wasn't what I wanted to think about when Dad was in town and I had to see him tomorrow.

Most of the day I felt trapped in Justin's sentence of silence. Becky and Crystal talked but I didn't really listen, anxiety knitting up inside me—I could hear the needles clicking—and my heart pumped away, like it was pounding out the rhythm on a base drum.

My hands shook when I got up to go out for lunch and I had a feeling that I was going to break into a full on panic attack soon.

I hadn't seen my parents for seven months. I didn't want to see them.

When I came back into the office, I looked at Justin, his head was down a little, and he had headphones in, listening to music as he worked, no doubt to drown me out if I spoke.

I'd got used to him being there when I'd needed someone. Being nice. He'd listened. God no one had ever listened to me before.

He understood too, 'cause of his Dad. I'd trashed that.

Awesome.

I sat down. There was no point messaging him again, he wasn't going to answer.

I sighed and got back on with my work. God, I wished he would be there tomorrow night.

The idea exploded in my head like a whole pan of popping corn breaking from the kernels all at once.

He'd wanted me to tell people we were together. The two things could collide tomorrow. If I asked him to come, there was no bigger statement; if I introduced him to my parents, it would make us front page news.

I looked over at him. He wasn't looking at me.

But how could I ask him when he wasn't even talking to me... and did he even like me now?

Justin

A knock hit the door. I looked up at Mom, and saw Robin do the same. We were sitting 'round the table eating dinner. It was eight already, too late for it to be someone selling stuff, and no one visited. Mom didn't have friends, she was too busy working, and she didn't let any of us encourage friends to call either. She wanted us all where she could see us, not on the streets where too many kids walked around with knives and guns. Or if she was working—where I could see them.

Jake glanced at me nervously as I stood up, like he was looking to his older brother for help. It was unusual for him. I gripped his shoulder for a moment as I lifted my other hand to tell Mum to sit back down as she stood too. "I'll go."

If it was trouble, it was better I was the one meeting it at the door. The conversation started up again behind me as Dillon said something that made Robin laugh. Dillon was still blind to the truth of life around here.

I shut the door behind me as I went into the hall. It was quiet and dark. I flicked the switch and the light blinked a couple of times before coming on.

I expected it to be a sales man, even if it was late, or Miriam from next door begging a cup of sugar, or something.

I looked through the spyglass.

Fuck.

It was Portia.

I pulled the door open. "What are you doing here?"

"I'm sorry."

She stood there, dressed in her silly woolen hat with its trailing

73

braids hanging over her ears. It was an out-of-office look. Her eyes glowed a strange gray in the white electric light seeping from the apartment. She breathed out, the steam of her breath misting in the cold air. The outdoor landing was open on the far side, and between the concrete pillars I could see the night sky. It was cloudy but the black was stained bright by the city lights.

My gaze came back to her. I rested my shoulder against the doorjamb and crossed my arms making a physical barricade, not just because I didn't want her in the apartment, but because I didn't want her in me...

"It's pointless, Portia." But what the fuck was she doing here, on her own, at night? She stood out like one of the Kardashians walking around in the middle of a *Call of Duty* game. Shit. It pulled at my need to protect the people I cared about.

I'd have to take her home.

"I don't know what else to say to you—" she started.

"Then say nothing." I wasn't interested in hearing her excuses. I turned to get my jacket. "I'll take you back."

"Justin…" She gripped my arm. "I want you to come to dinner with my parents. They're in New York. Would that redeem me? I'm sorry I wasn't ready to go public in the office but… I want you back. I miss you."

"Justin!" Mom's voice reverberated through the closed door behind us. "Justin!" Portia let go of me at the same moment the door opened.

Mom stopped dead, surprise knocking her off balance like a ten-pin, as if pretty, *white*, Portia, was a bowling ball.

I could hear the others talking and laughing at the table, but I couldn't see them.

I looked back. Portia's hand lifted to take off her hat, she looked nervous.

"Justin?" Mom called my attention back to her.

"Mom, this is Portia, the girl I've been seeing?" I hadn't told her it was over.

74

Portia gripped her woolen hat in front of her. "Hello, Mrs. Preston, I'm sorry to disturb you."

"Did this boy ask you over here and not tell me?" Mom looked embarrassed.

Portia's perfect, slightly British accent set her apart. It was clear she hadn't grown up anywhere near here.

"No, Mom—" I interjected… but she cut me off.

"Well, the boy shouldn't have asked you to come out here—not alone. It's not safe. You'd better come in and have something to eat, sweetheart?"

Shit.

"No, I—" Portia looked at me.

Before I could say yes or no, Mom said, "Have you eaten, child?"

Portia shook her head.

I raised my eyebrows.

"The girl hasn't eaten, Justin, let her eat…"

Mom thought I just wanted to go out, not that I was trying to avoid the torture of letting Portia in—that was all I'd wanted to do all week—I just didn't feel like being kicked again.

I sighed. I wasn't gonna win this. Mom didn't like the word no.

Mom's fingers closed over Portia's and her hat too as Portia gripped it tight. "We were just sitting down."

Cool.

"Well, now, my boy Justin's shocked me, I'm not gonna lie, and so you're gonna have to forgive my rudeness, sweetheart. I had no idea you were white, child. Your hand is freezing. Justin, how could you leave the girl on the step?" She kept talking as she led Portia away.

"Hey." I heard chairs scraping as Robin and Jake must have seen her and stood up. They'd be shocked too.

"This is Justin's girl. Get her a chair, Robin."

"Mom, her name's Portia." I corrected as I followed them in.

"See, I said he's shocked me. Here I am being rude to you, Portia. Justin, aren't you gonna take Portia's hat from her?" Mom smiled at Portia as she spoke to me.

I'd never gone out with a white girl. I'd never been inclined to. It was Portia I was into, her color hadn't counted. It still was just Portia I was into—even though she'd blanked me. '*He was in here when I came in!*' That had put everything in perspective.

Portia handed me the hat she'd still been clutching and our gazes caught, hers said sorry. Mine probably said—whatever.

I tucked her hat under my arm, so I could take her coat off her shoulders. I was angry with her, but I could be nice.

Robin had moved his chair beside Mom's for Portia and fetched a step-stool from the kitchen to sit on. He put it next to the chair he'd placed for Portia, glancing at me and grinning. I shoved his shoulder.

He laughed as Mom sat down but picked up the stool and moved it to the other side of the table so I could sit next to Portia.

Robin's face was a picture though. It would embarrass the hell out of him if I posted it on Facebook, he was all big eyed, and Jake's mouth was open.

I went and hung her coat up as Robin got himself acquainted, asking questions, and Mom dished Portia up a generous helping of the chicken and dumplings, ladling it on her plate, then adding rice and peas.

Robin asked how I'd met her.

"At work," I answered, before she could, as I sat next to her.

"So what do you do then, Portia?" Mom asked.

"I'm Mr. Rees's Personal Assistant. I manage his mail and his diary, and run errands and stuff." She ate a mouthful, chewing it in the prettiest way. She was just so perfect. Apart from the fact she didn't want anyone to know she'd been sleeping with me.

"Is that what you want to do all your life?" Mom said.

"I'd love to go into PR, but not at the moment, I'm happy where I am. It pays the bills, and it's an okay place to work."

"And your parents?" *Now there was a question.* "What do they do? Where do they live?"

"Mom, you don't have to interrogate her..."

"I'm just asking, child." She looked at me, then Portia. "You don't mind, do you, sweetheart?" It wasn't a question, Portia was being told she didn't care, but that was the force of my mom.

Portia shook her head. "I don't mind. They live in California for part of the year, and in Europe for some of it. My father owns a property business. He builds big complexes. He gave up having anything to do with the building ages ago though, now he pays other people to manage it."

Well that had all my family knocked over like pins.

Catching Robin looking at me, I smiled. He smiled back. Jake just looked like he wondered how the fuck his older brother had managed to hook up with a girl who was hot and loaded.

I didn't know. But then, it wasn't worth bragging about if the girl wanted to keep the whole thing a secret.

She kept talking to Mom, eating her dinner in between, and throwing a look at Robin every time he said something.

Jake kept eating, not looking at her now, as if looking at her was scary, but he wasn't scared of her, her beauty and her voice were just making him uncomfortable. She didn't fit in in our neighborhood.

Dillon's eyes were saucers, they watched her the whole time he ate, like I'd brought home an alien.

She leaned back once she'd finished her chicken, a little after the rest of us, as she'd started after us. She looked at Mom. "Thank you, Mrs. Preston, that was lovely."

Mom smiled. "I guess you'll be wanting some pudding now..."

"I—"

I knew Portia was going to say no. She didn't eat much. "She won't take no for an answer, you might as well give in." I whispered to Portia out the side of my mouth.

Mom started clearing plates. Robin, Dillon, and even Jake, got up to help her.

When the others carried the plates and dishes over to the kitchen counter, Portia's palm settled on my thigh. I looked at her. She didn't say anything, just looked back at me with imploring eyes. I didn't cover her hand, I kept my hands on the table. I wasn't gonna give in.

Mom had dished us up ice-cream for desert and added chocolate sprinkles for Dillon's sake. Portia ate it slowly smiling as even Jake found his voice and asked her a few questions, then Dillon found his voice too and bombarded her.

After we finished the ice-cream, I thought it was time to end this. "I better get you home," I stood up. She wasn't my girlfriend. It was time I got her out of here.

She looked at me, with hope, like she hadn't expected me to offer.

"Portia, this isn't the sort of neighborhood a woman walks around in on her own. I'll get your coat."

Mom looked at me as I passed her; perhaps finally realizing things weren't right. I didn't say anything, but I heard Portia stand up and say, "Thank you."

When I came back, I held her coat up and without looking at me she slipped her arms into the sleeves. I held out her hat. She took it from my hand, meeting my gaze but then looked away. I guess she didn't like what she saw.

"I'll see you later, Mom."

"You don't have to come home. I can walk Dillon to school." Robin spoke up before I could turn away. He grinned. I shook my head at him. But Mom was already nodding at me.

"Robin can do it, child. You don't need to come back. You stay out with Portia if you want to."

God, it was the first time she'd ever encouraged me to stay out... I nodded vaguely. I was coming back anyway.

I put my jacket on in the hall, and as soon as we stepped out the door, Portia started speaking.

"I'm really sorry, Justin. Can't you give me a second chance?"

I looked along the landing, walking next to her as the cold night air seeped through my jacket. "I don't do second chances,

Portia. I learned from Mom. She played the game for years, it got her nowhere."

"I—"

Voices carried on the polluted city air. There were guys in the stairwell. I gripped her arm. "Save it for later. Quiet now and do as I say." It sounded like there were half a dozen kids talking down there.

She pulled her arm free.

"Just say nothing," I repeated as we reached the stairs. "And keep moving."

She glanced at me but didn't speak as we descended. I saw eight kids down there. They weren't really kids but I classed them as kids, cause they acted like kids, playing follow the leader—*gangs*.

I stiffened, straightening, but tried to keep my shoulders relaxed. This was the only way out, we had to go through them, and the only way was to act like I didn't care. I didn't when I was on my own. I did with Portia next to me.

They looked up. I gave them a dismissive half smile, some of the faces I knew, but I didn't know their names. I didn't want to. I'd always kept my distance from the gangs around here. I'd stayed under their radar in my teens, and when I'd worked my way through University, I'd hardly been here. Now I just ignored them, and they did me… usually. But right now all these kids were looking at Portia, with eyes that asked, and gazes that hungered. Fuck.

I gripped her arm again as we neared them. None of them moved. "You gonna make way for me and my girl?" My other hand was firmly in my pocket, and I kept my pitch somewhere between unthreatening and insistent. But if they didn't move…

There was a pause as they all looked from her boots up to the bobble on the top of her woolen hat. I didn't stop; I kept moving; and kept her moving. Then finally they parted like the red sea for Moses. But I knew as we walked through them that their gazes had dropped to her ass.

79

I would willingly have hit every one of them. Dickheads!

I didn't speak until we got out of the stairwell and about ten yards away, in case the sound carried. Then I glanced at her. I was still gripping her arm. "You okay?"

She looked up. "Yeah, sorry. I shouldn't have come over, should I?"

Relaxing, I let go of her arm. "Nope, Portia. Bad idea to come here."

"Sorry." She looked ahead.

The streets were painted in the white light from the street lamps, but away from the light there were shadows everywhere. I didn't normally notice them, but with Portia... They were setting my nerves on edge.

She glanced at me again. "You're kind of attractive when you go all superhero."

Her expression was captured in the electric light, and it shot something hard and elemental through my gut. I was so into her, even though she could pretend I was nothing to do with her.

I looked away but inside I was laughing at her stupid comment, and I'd seen the light in her eyes that said she knew, and grabbed at hope again.

Her fingers closed about my arm, gripping my jacket, as we walked on. I didn't say anything. Neither did she.

On the subway train the car was quiet. I sat opposite her, elbows on my thighs and head down.

"You can talk to me."

I looked up and met her blue gaze but I didn't answer her.

She tried to look inside me. "I like your family. Your mum's nice. And your brothers..." The words died on her lips. I guessed she realized I wasn't gonna speak.

She looked at the adverts above my head.

My hands gripping together, I looked down again. She was such an anomaly, like she lived in her own universe.

"I wish my mum was like yours..." Her words carried across

the car in a wistful whisper, no longer spoken to me but just said into the air. I looked at her again.

She was so locked up at work, but here, now, when she was just with me, she was a girl, finding her way, trying to work stuff out on her own... *On her own...*

Most girls weren't completely alone... Was I judging her too hard? Was my vision clouded by my life—my dad? She'd walked out on everything she'd ever known a year ago, and come here to start a new life. That must have been tough—scary.

I watched as she still looked up. She'd had courage to do that. No wonder she didn't put herself out there so readily.

Bullshit.

I got up and swapped seats, dropping into the one next to her. "Okay, spill, why are you such an idiot? Why hide what we had going on?"

Her gaze turned to me. "I didn't mean to, it just happened. I didn't know what to say..."

I stared at her a moment. "Because..."

Her answer came out angry. "Because I don't know how to do this!"

I twisted to face her, my knee lifting to rest against the arm of her seat. "Do what, Portia?"

"Oh, I don't know, I don't even know who me is anymore." Her hand pulled off her hat. There were tears in her eyes. She looked up at the adverts again. "I'm sorry..."

"For what?"

Her head spun to face me once more. "Don't be such a douchebag, Justin. What? Why? I told you, I don't know! I give up, okay. I get it. You don't want to be with me anymore."

There was a sudden lurch low in my belly that slipped to grip in my groin.

I did.

Without thinking, I touched her cheek, then leaned to press a firm quick kiss on her lips before answering over them. "I do,

81

actually, but only if you're gonna walk in to work tomorrow and tell everyone you're with me."

She didn't speak but her lips parted like she was searching for words.

"Look, Portia, I know... I know your parents let you down, your boyfriend let you down—life let you down. But I won't, not deliberately. You can be brave with me. I know how it feels to be on the other end of that. I won't do it to you, or anyone. Okay? But it's gonna take courage. You've got to come out of your shell at work. I'm not joining you in your double life. Take the shields down, baby."

A tear rolled onto her cheek, then it was followed by another, and then she stood up and moved, shifting to sit on my knee. I held her and she buried her face in my neck.

I didn't say anything as she sobbed her heart out, just held her, wondering how long the Portia I'd been making fun of at work had been damning up all this emotion. Probably from the day she'd walked out and had to lock all her fear and loneliness up so tight no one was ever gonna spot it.

I ran my fingers through her hair.

"You okay? We've got to get off in a moment." She nodded, sniffing and wiping her nose on her sleeve, then she got up.

When we walked back to her place, I slung my arm over her shoulders and tucked her in close.

When we got to her apartment block, she took out her key. "Are you coming in? I'd like you to, if you want to?

"I mean you're right about me, I do hide, because if I let me out, I think... I'm gonna get hurt." She took a breath, her gaze holding mine. "But when it's you and me—I don't feel like that. I'm not afraid when you're around...

"Will you come out with me tomorrow, to have dinner with my parents? And will you stay with me tonight?" The heart-felt plea shone from her eyes too.

How could I say no? I didn't even want to say no.

"Yes, to both, Portia. If tomorrow morning you walk into the office with me and tell them we've got something going on."

She smiled. "What like tell them we're going out?"

"Yeah, tell them we're *going out*," I said it with a preppy accent.

She turned to the door and slipped her key in the lock, then twisted it, opening the door. I walked in behind her and took her hand as we started climbing the stairs—memories, echoes, of the sessions we'd had upstairs spun in my head.

Abstinence made the heart grow fonder—more hungry.

I'd missed her.

Her hand slipped from mine, so she could open the lock of her own door. When we were in there I pushed it shut, turned her and pressed her back against the wood, kissing her with a hunger that came from low in belly.

There was something like a clamp about my heart, holding it in a vice like grip as she kissed me back.

She wasn't just perfect, she was precious, and she needed someone like me to let her know it so she had the courage to step out of her jammed up terror filled world.

Chapter Nine

Portia

It was the weirdest, most wonderful thing to wake up to my alarm buzzing with my head resting on Justin's chest for a pillow, and his arm around me.

He stretched, yawning. I turned onto my belly and rested my fingers on his chest, looking up at him. I could get lost in his brown eyes.

"Happy?" he asked, his fingers running through my hair.

"Yeah. You?"

"Very." His lips parted in a huge smile.

"You go shower," I told him. "I'll make you coffee and breakfast."

"Breakfast? What's for breakfast?"

"Wait and see, go shower."

When he came back I was at the counter, the coffee steaming in two cups, filling the room with a fresh aroma, while I fried off his pancakes. His fingers slipped across my belly as he stood behind me, and his lips kissed the sensitive skin behind my ear. I tried flipping the pancake and nearly dropped it when he bit me. "Justin!"

He didn't shift an inch, just gripped my belly harder holding me against him as he whispered to my ear. "When you're at work, think about this, think about how, when we get home, I'm gonna have you leaning against the counter before we go out with your parents…"

I turned around and his hands slipped away, but then my head was braced between his long fingers, and his mouth came down on mine. I think it was one of the best kisses I'd ever had, it made my belly go all mushy and my legs weak.

Then without protesting at all, I had intended to, I turned back to the hot ring and tipped his fifth pancake on to the plate, before holding out the maple syrup. "Here, eat up, I'm going for a shower."

"You're not eating?" He took the maple syrup.

"I already ate one, and I'm still full up from your mum's chicken."

He laughed as I dodged out the room, before he could catch me and pull me in for another kiss.

We walked to work together, holding hands, but as we got nearer to the office, my heart started playing base beat rhythms. Shit, how was I gonna do this? I'd kept *me* locked away for over a year. They knew the front I put on, not the girl behind it.

Justin had called his mom this morning when we'd left my place, to check she'd got to work okay. Then he'd called Robin to check his other brothers had got to school okay. No one knew that about him at work…

Just 'cause I was going out with Justin didn't mean they all had to know the rest of my shit.

When he got to the reception, Justin looked at me. "Stairs or lift?"

"Stairs." I was still a coward, the stairs gave me a few more minutes to avoid this—or a few more minutes of torture. Maybe not such a good idea. But as we climbed, his fingers slipped in between mine and gripped hard, offering reassurance.

"Sorry I'm such an idiot."

"You aren't an idiot, Portia, you're perfect. Just relax a little."

"Okay." I tried but my heart was playing a race against time in my chest. I felt like I was going to faint when he opened the door and pulled me through, still hanging on to my hand.

When we walked into the open plan room, several people looked, but not because we were anything special, just out of habit. But instead of looking away, they kept looking and eyebrows lifted.

Becky's mouth dropped open when she spotted us, and her eyes widened as she stood up.

Justin said, "Hey," to her as we passed, ignoring her reaction, and simply walking me to my chair.

Gentleman that he was, he let go of my hand, giving me a big smile, and lifted his fingers to the shoulders of my coat to help me take it off.

I sat down staring at him like a fool. He leaned over and kissed my lips, whispering as heat and air across my mouth, "Just so there's no confusion, and they know we're dating."

There was that odd delicious feeling in my belly again.

The instant he walked away and around to his desk, Becky and Crystal came over. Justin winked at me before he sat.

"Oh my God. You and Justin!" Crystal exclaimed

"Did you lie to me the other day, or was it just starting off?" Becky eyed me with suspicion.

"I just wasn't sure where we were," I answered, "But yeah, now we are officially seeing each other." It actually felt really good to say it. "I'm going out with Justin."

I got a hug from Becky and Crystal, then they walked away as the sub-editor, Hilary, headed over, no doubt about to say, get on with your work. She turned when she saw them walk off. I had a ton of letters to get done for Mr. Rees. I put my earphones in to discover the first one was to that solicitor in Oregan, denying the paternity case.

God, everyone had thought Justin was a sleaze—Mr. Rees was the sleaze.

I went into my email and typed. 'Are you going home to get some clothes to wear out to dinner tonight? You're going to need a suit and tie.'

It felt really good to have Justin there at the end of an email again.

'I haven't got a suit, baby, no point in me going back home.'

I wanted to laugh, the guy was so not like me, so not my type, and yet... He was perfect too.

'Then we're going shopping at lunch time, I'll buy you some stuff.'

'I'm not your charity case. I'll buy my own stuff.'

'Cool, you pay, I'll pick! :D'

'Not a Tommy Hilfiger shirt and Versace suit though, something I can afford!'

'Okay :) Twelve?'

'Twelve.'

'It's going to be a long morning.'

'It's gonna be a long day; just thinking about you over the counter, winking face'

'Well stop thinking!!' I looked up, and he leaned around his screen, smiling at me and laughing. I smiled too, a full on smile. I don't think I normally smiled that much at work.

Portia

Work had been weird, but weird in a good way. I'd felt Justin's presence all day. Because of what he'd said in the morning, I was thinking about him constantly.

I had somebody on my side. Team Portia. I wasn't fighting life alone anymore.

We'd gone down to the mall at lunchtime, and he'd got a plain black jacket and a pair of skinny black chinos. I'd picked a very basic white shirt to go with them and a narrow burgundy tie. I was going to wear my burgundy dress, so I thought it would look cool to match.

"Do I need the shades too, to go totally men-in-black?" he'd asked, picking up a pair, like he'd need them in the restaurant. Justin's sense of humor was foolish at times; but he was just living life while I'd spent a year hiding from it.

I'd flashed him a smile, took the shades off him, and put them back on the shelf.

I'd smiled a ton of times today.

Once, when he'd been joking with Becky, I'd overheard and looked up, caught his gaze, and, God, there was a massive transmission of information between us, like it downloaded in a rush. It poured right into my heart, sending tremors to my belly.

We were good together.

I kept telling myself that as we walked into the restaurant later. We'd stopped in a bar around the corner and had a drink for courage and I was now a little intoxicated, and anxious—terrified. *We're good together.* The words whispered through my head. My parents wouldn't think so.

The maitre d' had given our coats to someone at the door, and now we trailed behind him as he led us across the busy room, weaving about tables.

My sweaty palm pressed against Justin's as his hand gripped mine, our fingers threaded. I wanted to wipe my palms on the skirt of my burgundy dress, but it was silk and that would ruin it. And besides, I didn't want to let go of Justin's hand.

I caught our reflection in a mirror as we passed it. Justin looked good in his jacket and tie, and we complemented each other. *We are good together.*

"Portia." I turned to see Dad stand up, and then Mum. They both looked at Justin. It wasn't the color of his suit or tie they noticed; it was the color of his skin. It wasn't that they were racist, it was just that they wouldn't think he was the right guy for *me*…

"Mum, Dad, I told you I was bringing a friend. This is Justin Preston." I took a breath, I had to do this. I had to give him full credit. "We've been dating; he's my boyfriend."

Justin let go of my hand and reached out. "Mrs. Hemming, it's nice to meet you."

Maybe I should've warned them he was black, but I didn't think it mattered. Justin was Justin, the color of his skin was irrelevant. Mum stared at him for a second or two, then finally took his hand and shook it. "Justin."

When she let his hand go, he turned to my dad, and held it out again. "Mr. Hemming."

"Justin." My dad's acknowledgement was short and sharp. Then he threw Mum a look that said it all. *What the hell.*

They could think what they wanted. I was done with their fake life, and their stupid facade.

Justin pulled out my seat before the maitre d' could, and helped me sit, pushing the chair back in.

"Well then, what brings you to New York?" I asked as Justin sat. My hands shook and my stomach felt like Jell-o.

"Can we not come to the city to see our daughter?" Dad opened.

Except… they weren't visiting me, they'd come to shop and sent me an invite to visit them.

"Is there some fashion thing going on Mum?" I looked at Dad then. "Or do you have some particular friend in town that you wanted to visit." I couldn't resist the dig. I knew there was something that must have brought them here, it wouldn't be me.

"It's going to be like that then, is it Portia?"

"Perhaps."

Justin's fingers gripped my thigh beneath the table, offering reassurance—solidarity. Go team Portia.

The conversation dropped to silence.

"Your menus." Having handed them out, the waiter began explaining every dish in complex detail, trying to get our taste buds flowing—mine were numb.

When he walked away, Mum said over the top of her menu, "So what do you like to eat, Justin?" She was speaking to him like he was a child.

"Mum, Justin works on all the photographic images at work, he worked his way through university. He can pick what he wants from a menu without you prompting."

"I didn't mean—" she shot back, but I cut her off as Justin's fingers rubbed up and down my thigh.

"Leave us to decide what we do and don't want, Mum." The conversation died.

After the waiter had taken our order, Dad tried again. "So what have you been up to, Portia?"

My instinct was to cut back, *what have you been up to?* I didn't say it, I figured I ought to at least try and be a little nice, they had asked me out after all. "Working, not much else."

"Do you do much shopping, or—"

"I just work, Dad, there's nothing wrong with that. Remember when you used to do it?"

"Portia." My name was the barked order I'd grown up with that said stop.

My lips compressed and I just stared at them. It seemed I couldn't stop myself. This was torture. I wished I hadn't come.

"Justin," Mum looked at him, ignoring my irritability, "so what is it you do?"

"He airbrushes, Margery, takes the inches off and adds the six packs." Dad answered for Justin like Justin couldn't speak for himself; trying to come across as though Mr. popularity-Hemming knew everything.

"He doesn't, we work on a sports magazine, Dad, the people we cover are hot anyway, we don't need to airbrush them."

Justin's fingers clawed a little on my thigh, and I heard him take a breath, before he spoke. "Actually, babe, I do, sometimes. I get rid of all the blemishes and stuff, they all want to look good." He looked at my dad. "But mainly, Mr. Hemming, I cut images to fit, overlay stuff, change the color contrasts and structure sometimes, and build text over them, and make up fun images to pull articles together." He shrugged when he finished speaking. Dad looked at Justin like he didn't know what to say.

Mum dived in. "So do you like what you do, Justin?" It was said in a tone of voice that implied he shouldn't. The work we did was below either of them.

"Uh huh."

"But have you plans for the future?" Dad asked. "I mean, it's not something that's ever going to make you successful…"

Justin shrugged. "Surely success is dependent on what you want to achieve. If what I want to achieve is a good picture for the front cover tomorrow, then I'm successful. I've achieved it." He smiled at Dad, not at all intimidated.

I smiled too, relaxing for the first time. I needed Justin's chilled logic in my life.

I slipped my hand underneath the table and gripped his thigh too, then slipped my fingers up and brushed his crotch. His whole body jolted and he coughed.

"You okay?" Dad asked.

"Yes, thank you Mr. Hemming. I'm just gonna go use the restroom." I looked up at him, feeling like someone was ripping my right arm off when he stood up.

His fingers brushed my cheek gently, only for a second, as his brown eyes said, *you'll be okay*.

He was only five paces away when Dad started. "Really, Portia, a black boy!"

"How could you, Portia?" Mum added. I hated her siding with Dad when he was such a cheating bastard…

"Where does he even come from?"

"A neighborhood in the Bronx, Dad."

"Portia!"

"He doesn't have any prospects…" Mum added.

"Why does he need prospects, Mum? He's good fun, he looks hot, he's nice, and he's good in bed…" I checked the things off on my fingers, then looked a Dad. "Oh yeah, and he's loyal, 'cause his Dad messed around…" I threw him a smile.

"There is no need for that." It was Mum who answered, the wounded party, but the wounded party who'd quite happily turned a blind eye and pocketed all his money.

"Portia, you should think about this, before you let yourself get in too deep. I know you came to New York because you were angry with us, but there's no need to try and shock us…"

"Dating Justin isn't anything to do with you, or what happened…"

"No…" It was said as if there was no way I could really want to be with Justin.

I hated my parents. They were bigots. How the hell had I come from them? Really I should divorce them. Why couldn't you divorce your parents, and have their names taken off your birth certificate?

"Hey baby." I looked up as Justin came back, and he bent down and kissed my cheek. I guessed he knew they'd been talking about him. He sat down, and reached for his drink.

"So, Justin, Portia says you come from the Bronx…" Dad said it as if he expected Justin to launch into a confession of murder or something…

"Yep."

"And your family?"

Justin smiled at him. "Yep, they come from there too."

"And do you have brothers and sisters, what does your mother do?" Mum took over.

He glanced at me, recognizing that she didn't mention his Dad, and obviously guessing I'd said something. I gave him a sorry smile, but he shook his head to say he didn't care. Then he looked at Mum and answered, "I have three brothers, ranging from eight to seventeen. And Mom's a nurse in an old folks home, she works hard to keep us, always has. I have a lot of respect her. Despite everything she's been through, she has a lot of love and she keeps us all together."

Well that shut my parents up. I smiled smugly at Dad. Then looked at Mum. I should feel sorry for her, but she was weak and soulless as a Mum. I couldn't feel sorry for her. She'd never given me anything that Justin's Mum gave him. Love.

Justin put his hand on my thigh again, but this time palm up.

I slipped my hand under the table and gripped it. The gesture said—*I got you.*

I changed the subject to safe talk. "So how's the business going, Dad?" That would keep him talking for an hour.

When our first course arrived Dad was still talking. I ate my parma ham and orange salad, while Justin got all messy with his stringy melted deep fried cheese thing, both of us nodding at Dad, but not really listening.

When they came to take the plates, Dad ordered another bottle of wine, and I took the opportunity to swap the conversation over to Mum. "What have you been up to? Have you got anything planned with your friends?" She went on to talk about this party they were planning for spring, to raise money for a local charity.

Her life was so false. She made out to the world her marriage was perfect. Her friends probably knew the truth anyway. Dad wasn't discrete.

They brought over the main courses. Justin had gone for steak. I'd picked the sea bass. The conversation dried again as we started eating, but then the notes of a *Jay-Z* song rose from Justin's jacket pocket. He let his knife and fork fall, and his eyebrows lifted as he reached for his cell.

People around the restaurant started staring, judging. Dad glared.

Justin pulled it out and answered, "Mom?"

"Really? Shit!"

"What the fuck?" He stood up as he talked, his napkin sliding to the floor. I put my cutlery down.

"Alright. I'm coming." His voice was sharp and agitated, and his hand lifted to lay on top of his head, then fell.

"No. I'm coming."

"Don't worry."

He ended the call. I stood, but he lifted his hand to say stay.

"It's Jake, he's got himself into trouble. He's at the hospital. I'm sorry, Portia. I've got to go. Someone's stabbed him."

"Oh my God." I didn't know what to think.

Justin looked at Mum and Dad. "I'm sorry Mr. and Mrs. Hemming. Thanks for dinner, but I've got to go, it's my kid brother. It was nice meeting you." He turned away and my stupid parents didn't say a word.

"Wait." I dropped my napkin on the table. "I'll come with you."

Justin looked at me, his eyes focusing for the first time—with gratitude. "Thanks. I'll go get your coat and my jacket…"

He was walking away when I looked back at Mum and Dad. "Sorry. Thanks for dinner."

I was going to turn away but Mum caught hold of my wrist. "Darling, you cannot really be serious about this boy…"

I took a breath and suddenly I knew. "I can be, and I am, Mum." There was this huge ball of feeling all wrapped up inside me for Justin. I was serious about him—really serious—and I didn't even feel afraid knowing it. I was in a fairytale again.

"Well don't expect anything from me, if he's after money," Dad threw.

I looked at him. I didn't feel sorry for myself anymore, I felt sorry for him. "He's not, Dad. Not at all. You can think what you like but he's not, and if you want to see me again you're going to have to accept I'm with Justin now. Goodnight."

I didn't wait to hear what else they had to say. I turned away, thinking about how warm and welcoming Justin's mum and brothers were… And now Jake was hurt. It would hurt them all.

Chapter Ten

Portia

Justin didn't really speak to me when we left the restaurant and walked to the subway. It was as if he didn't even know I was there. But I knew he did know, and I knew he needed me. I touched his hand. It was shaking, but he didn't grip mine, instead his hand lifted and his fingers ran over his hair about four times as he whispered. "Bullshit."

I didn't know what to say. There was nothing I could say to help. But last year, I'd walked out on a load of shit and tried to cope alone—he wouldn't want to be alone.

I kept pace with him, hurrying as he walked fast.

"Fricking shit," he breathed.

I didn't answer.

On the subway train, when I sat down, he took the seat facing me and bent over, his hands gripping his head. There were only a few other people in the car but they weren't near us. His fingers spread bracing his head as he looked at the floor.

What could I do? I didn't want to intrude on his feelings, but he looked in agony. I wanted to touch him, to reassure him. To try and make it better; even though there was nothing I could do or say that would do that.

Jake had been stabbed and no words were going to change it…

Shit, the truth hit me in the face with a punch. Justin's brother had been stabbed, he could be bleeding to death right now…

I got up and moved across the car to sit next to him. I put my hand on his back. It jolted. He was crying. "Justin…" His name came out on a breath. I held him. "I'm sorry."

He sat up straight, suddenly, so I had to let go, but then his arm came about me, as his other hand wiped at his eyes, then his nose. "Sorry, Portia. This night was about you."

"Don't worry about me. I'm just worried about you… and your brother."

"Fuck, Jake was always the one. I knew he was the one… He was so quiet, but he talked to Robin, and I thought Robin… Shit. What the fuck was he doing?"

His frustration sliced through me. "Don't go in there angry. You can't undo anything, and I know how easy it is to get sucked into things, different things, but…"

He looked at me his brown eyes shining in the white light of the car. "I know that, I've fought like mad to keep them all out of it, but it's hard walking that line, and for months now there's been this feeling in my gut about Jake, but I didn't do anything. I didn't know what to do…" His hand gripped my shoulder and it was painful, but then he let go and bent over again, gripping his head in his hands. "Fuck. Why didn't I do something?"

I rubbed his back in a pathetic attempt to give comfort, but I could hardly say it would be okay, I didn't know. I didn't even know how badly Jake was injured. I didn't even know if Justin knew.

When we walked into the hospital, we were holding hands. He'd gripped mine the whole way from the subway station. He glanced at me as the glass doors of the reception slid open. "Thanks for coming with me?"

I smiled. "I'm right here."

He let go of my hand as he walked up to reception, and took a deep breath before saying. "I've come to see Jake Preston, my family's already here. He's my brother. Where is he?"

96

The woman looked at her screen and typed Jake's name in. She looked up. "Your family will be up in the waiting area. Turn right, take the elevator to the second, then go left through the double doors, it's along the corridor, follow the signs for ICU, and it's on the right."

"You're going to have to write that down," I answered. "We're both in shock."

She immediately drew a little map on a piece of paper and gave it to me. "There you go. They'll be a nurse up there to advise you." She gave Justin a look as he turned away. She was black too, but I still felt like she was judging him, weighing up whether he was part of the gang or not.

I gave her a twisted smile. *Not.* But surely she could tell. Justin was still wearing his suit jacket, and he was a whole pile of caring. But I hadn't known he was so caring either, not until I'd got close.

Justin had already gone. "Thank you," I said to the woman, then rushed after him. "Justin!"

I caught up with him after he'd pressed the elevator button. He looked back at me, his eyes full of agony. "I want to go and see him, but another part of me just wants to walk away and not deal with this... It's my fault."

I gripped his hand as he watched the lights flashing through the floor numbers showing the elevator's descent.

"It's not your fault... You can't be everywhere at once..."

The elevator doors opened. We walked in and his hand slipped from mine so he could press the button.

He stood against the wall, away from me, resting his head back against the gleaming metal.

I felt for him, I didn't have any brothers or sisters, I couldn't be in his shoes, but I could imagine, and I knew what if felt like to lose love.

When the elevator stopped he came to life, moving suddenly. Then he almost ran the route through the warren of corridors, until we saw his brother, Robin.

He was sitting on a chair, in an alcove set back in the corridor with his head in his hands. His white T-shirt was covered in blood.

My stomach turned over inside my belly, bile rising in my throat. Shit.

Robin sat up, and tears rolled down his cheeks.

"Robin! He's not dead?" Anguish stole Justin's voice.

Robin shook his head. He didn't stand up, he looked too shaken. "He's in surgery. Mom's taken Dillon to get a drink. What the frick did I do, Justin?"

Justin sat next him and drew him into a harsh hug. "You did nothing. It's my fault. I shouldn't have left it down to you."

"I've asked him about gangs, and he never said a word..." There was a desperate plea in Robin's eyes. I understood Justin's relationship with his brothers then, he wasn't only their big brother—he was like their dad.

"Seriously, it's not your fault, it's mine. I should've made him swear to me he hadn't got caught up in anything."

My hands slipped into my coat pockets. Love hung around them. It was thick in the air. Selfishly, I thought of my parents. They would never be this distressed if anything happened to me...

Robin's head pressed into Justin's shoulder as he started crying again. "It's okay." Justin laid his hand on his brother's head. "It's not your fault."

I turned as the double doors into the corridor swung open. "Mrs. Preston." Her skin had a grayish tone, and her eyes were full of pain. Dillon gripped her hand, but even as I noticed it, his hand pulled free.

"Justin!" The kid ran at his big brother as if Justin being here could put this whole mess right. Robin straightened wiping his eyes, as Justin turned to catch Dillon's charge and pulled him up onto his bent leg. Dillon hugged him.

"It's okay. Don't worry," Justin said in a low voice.

Robin looked at his mum, guilt burning in his eyes.

I could see she didn't think he was guilty. This family didn't judge. My heart reached out. I wanted to hug her, but I'd only met her yesterday.

Dillon's head was buried in Justin's shoulder and he was crying as Robin had done.

Justin looked at his mum, eyes wide and questioning. "How is he?"

"There was so much blood," Robin whispered.

Justin's hand slipped over Dillon's ear, and his Mum said, "Robin!" Then she looked at Justin. "They are looking for internal injuries before they stitch him up."

"He was in the stairwell," Robin said. "Just left there. He was late and I went looking for him. He was on the landing. Lying in all this blood. Unconscious. He must have called for help... No one... I... Oh shit, Justin..."

Justin looked at his mum. "How long is he gonna be in surgery?"

"They didn't say."

What could Justin do?

But I could help them. I looked at Robin. "Robin, why don't Dillon and I go out and get you some clean clothes. You don't want to sit here like that." He looked at me as if only now he realized he was covered in Jake's blood. He must have held Jake when he'd found him.

These brothers were starting to claim pieces of my heart.

"What size are you? Small..."

"Yeah."

"And jeans?"

"28" long."

I turned to Justin, his eyes were wide. "Are you okay if I go? I mean, I think it would be good for Dillon too."

"But on your own?"

"The Mall we passed was only 'round the corner. I'm not going far, and it's a busy street, we'll be okay."

Justin's hand had slipped to Dillon's shoulder. Dillon sat upright staring at me.

"Do you want to come with me, Dillon, maybe we can find a Mackie Ds and get you something to eat, yeah? I bet you didn't eat dinner did you?" He shook his head. I held out my hand. "Come on then, let's go get your brother some clean clothes."

Dillon slipped off Justin's leg, and his hand came up and gripped mine as I looked at Justin again. Gratitude weighted his gaze.

"Thanks." He mouthed rather than said.

He needed the time alone with Robin and his mum, so they could talk without frightening Dillon.

I nodded. "Come on then, Dillon."

Portia

Shopping with Dillon was fun. The kid was funny. He *was* hurting, but kids dealt with stuff in different ways to adults, and getting out of the hospital was the best thing for him. He shelved everything for an hour, and was just a kid—a kid who hadn't looked a nightmare in the face a little while before.

He chose Robin a black shirt, and picked out Robin's favorite style of Levis. Then when we walked past a sweet shop he happened to see his favorite watermelon sweets. I think my generous plastic card and I were getting taken for a ride, but I didn't mind, I had the money.

At Mackie Ds, we stopped for cheese burgers, fries and shakes.

Then we were on our way back to the hospital.

Dillon went quiet from the moment we left the mall. He'd been constantly talking the rest of the time, always about his brothers, and mostly about Justin. Though he kept flying back to mentioning Jake, like he kept remembering Jake was in a room nearby being operated on…

When we came through the door into the corridor outside the ICU ward, I saw them all sitting together. His Mum was leaning back looking our way. Justin was leaning back too with his legs splayed. He'd taken his jacket off and loosened his tie, so the knot hung a couple of inches below his collar. He'd released the top button of his shirt too. Beside him, Robin was leaning forward, his fingers gripping either side of his head as his elbows rested on his thighs.

Dillon's hand slipped from mine. He had the shopping bag, and he ran straight for Robin. "We got you a nice shirt, and Levis…"

Justin's gaze caught mine and his eyebrows lifted.

I knew they never normally bought Levis. I just smiled.

"Thanks." Robin half-heartedly took the bag.

I looked at him. "Robin, Dillon probably needs the restroom, we had a burger and shake. Why don't you take him and go change?" I'd worked these brothers out already, there was one thing they all had in common—they looked out for one another. Looking after Dillon would take Robin's mind off himself.

His head came up, and he looked at me. His eyes full of sorrow and doubt, but I'd touched the right nerve.

"Thanks," he said again as he stood up. "Come on Dillon." His hand gripped Dillon's shoulder and turned him. "Little bro."

When they walked away, I took the seat next to Justin.

He gripped my hand, like he'd been longing to do it the whole time I'd been gone.

"How is he, do you know?"

"Not yet—"

"Jake is still in surgery," his mum finished.

That long… That was bad, surely.

"Do you know how it happened?"

Justin

Do you know how it happened? Portia asked the question Robin, Mom and I, had been throwing around between us for the hour Portia had been gone. How? Why? The only one who knew was Jake, and Jake was in surgery fighting for his life. He couldn't speak.

I slotted my fingers between Portia's. "We don't know anything."

"Do you think it was those boys we walked through last night?"

A sharp jolt of anger caught in my belly because that was what

I had thought. Had they been there, hanging around, to get at Jake? "I don't know." I wished I did know.

God, I couldn't believe how angry I was. I wanted to smash up the hospital when the hospital had done nothing wrong. They were saving his life.

But frick... Jake.

I was still numb. I was living in another universe and looking in through a window at this one. I wasn't in my head. I gripped Portia's hand harder. I couldn't believe she'd taken Dillon away...

Portia...

Self-interested, stuck-up, Portia had helped my mom by looking after my kid brother. I had got the girl wrong. Right now she was my pathway back to sanity.

Shit Jake. What the frick were you doing?

I tipped my head back against the wall and shut my eyes. *Lord, I know I don't pray but if you are up there, I'm praying now, and not for me, for Jake. Save him. He doesn't deserve this. I let him down. Don't let him die.*

A tear rolled from my right eye. Portia wouldn't be able to see it. Its path tracked down my cheek. I didn't wipe it away. My tears would prove to God how much I cared. The Man had to save Jake. *What can I give you? I'll give you anything if you save my brother.*

My eyes stayed shut and air pulled into my lungs. I let it out. *Come on, Jake, live.* Now I started sending my vibes through the air to him, willing him to fight, and live.

"Mrs. Preston?"

My eyes shot open. There was a guy in a green suit standing before us, his hands hung at his sides, and he had a stupid green hat on. Mom nodded.

"Can I have a word?"

Oh shit. Was the guy going to say Jake hadn't survived?

Mom stood up, and I stood up too, without even thinking.

"This is Jake's brother," Mom said.

"Will you come with me?" He held his hand out.

I was still gripping Portia's, and she'd stood too. "Is it okay if my girlfriend comes?"

"Yes of course, if you wish her to be there."

I wished her to be there. "Yes." Portia pressed close to my shoulder and hugged my arm, offering comfort and reassurance. She didn't succeed, but I cared more for her for trying.

The guy led us to a tiny room. Inside it there were four low cushioned chairs. He sat on one. Mum sat next to him. I was still gripping Portia's hand as she sat next to me. We all leaned forward, desperate to hear.

"Mrs. Preston, your son survived the surgery, but his spleen has ruptured, so we've had to remove it and repair areas of his bowel. The stab wound didn't damage any other organs but we're keeping him in ICU until we're sure he's okay."

"ICU?" I echoed, surely that meant things were bad.

"The Intensive Care Unit. Don't worry, he's not in any immediate risk, but the next twenty-four hours are crucial, if he survives those, then he should be okay."

Emotion thrashed around in my chest smashing me up, like I wanted to smash the world up. Jake...

"Can we see him?" Mom asked.

"In a little while. Give him a chance to settle." The guy took a breath. "Have you thought about how you'll cover the bills?"

I shut my eyes for an instant. We didn't have that sort of money. It was going to take us a lifetime to pay this off.

"I'll sort it," Portia whispered quietly.

I looked at her, my fingers catching even tighter about hers. "It's not your responsibility."

"I know, but I want to, I have the money. I had a trust fund. It paid out when I was twenty-one. I've never touched it. I wanted Dad to know I could support myself, but… this… I want to use it. "

I looked at Mom, she would hate the idea.

"Let me, please." Portia didn't give her a chance to argue. "Mrs. Preston. It's nothing to me… Let me help you?" Mom opened her

103

mouth to protest, but Portia carried on. "The money is just sitting in a bank. Let me use it please. It'll take you years to pay the bills back. I can pay it now and you won't need to worry..."

Mum's eyes looked defeated, she didn't want to have to say yes, and yet she had to. We didn't have the money.

"I'd be grateful, Portia. Thank you."

Oh my God. What the fuck was going on today? Mom looked at Portia with eyes that apologized for saying yes. She'd always hated help. She was a fighter, she did stuff for herself, worked it out, got through it... But now...

I looked at the doctor. "You'll tell us as soon as we can see him..."

"As soon as, but you'll need to be patient a little longer."

The man stood and said, "If you haven't got any more questions?" as if he was really telling us not to have any more 'cause he needed to get back to work.

"Nope," I answered.

"No," Mum echoed.

Portia looked from Mom to me, then up at the doctor.

"Very well then. We'll keep you informed." With that, the guy was gone.

Portia stood up. "I'm gonna go down to the reception and sort out the payment."

I stood too. "Portia, you don't have to do that..."

"I know, but I want to. I'll be back soon. Mrs. Preston, you can concentrate on Jake then."

I turned back to Mom when Portia went out, though really I wanted to go with Portia. "You okay?"

She stood up. I rested my hand on her shoulder and she turned into me, holding me for a moment.

She wasn't tactile. She was a fighter, not a comforter. This wasn't usual for her.

I sighed and put both my arms around her for a moment. She didn't cry. She'd stopped crying when Dad left.

"He'll be okay," I said, I wanted to believe it.

104

She pulled away from me and looked up, the light in her eyes dulled by pain. "Robin, is probably finished changing—he's gonna be wondering where we are, and Dillon will worry."

I nodded.

I reached past her and pulled the door open for her so she could walk ahead of me, but in the corridor my gaze reached for Portia. She was gone.

Robin was sitting in a chair in the waiting area, and Dillon was beside him holding out a book he must have got from a toy box somewhere.

Robin stood up. "Where have you been?" He was scared. I set a hand on his shoulder. Mom gave Dillon a hug. "Jake's out of surgery. He's okay, but now it's just wait and see." I turned. "Mom, I'm going after Portia."

She nodded, before focusing on Dillon again. He was holding the book up for her to read.

My pace increased with every step. I wanted to run, and just get out of here. I'd failed.

As I stood in the elevator, I bashed my head back against the metal about three times, trying to knock out all the emotion tumbling around in my head. I didn't succeed.

Portia stood by the counter, leaning on it, filling in some form when I got down to reception. I leaned on the counter next to her. I wanted to hold her so tight she'd get squished.

She was filling out bank information. "You don't have to do that, Portia."

She glanced at me. "I know, but I want to, and that's the end of that conversation. Don't upset your mum."

She carried on writing. She was right. But having to take money off her was crap. It shifted everything between us.

I sighed as she swirled her signature and handed the form to the woman behind the counter. She read it over, then looked up. "Thank you. It all looks fine."

"Thanks," Portia answered before turning to me, her head

tipping a little to the side, like she felt my annoyance and didn't know what to do. But frick, I didn't know what to do either. My brother was upstairs in ICU, and I was taking thousands of dollars off my girlfriend, who'd only agreed to be my girlfriend yesterday!

But I wanted to kiss her. I just wanted to escape into her.

"Do you want to go back up?" she asked. "Or do you want some fresh air for a minute?"

Air suddenly seemed like gold. "Air."

She gripped my hand and pulled me. I was unraveling—falling apart. I needed to get outside the door. It was dark, but the darkness was bleached white from the streetlights.

She pulled me to one side, and into the shadow thrown by some plant, then she lifted up onto her toes, and pressed a kiss against my jaw as her arms reached around my neck. I held her too, my arms a tight band, hanging on in a hurricane; and then I cried like a jackass. But it was the fear tied so tight in me slipping out into her. She never lifted her head, didn't say a word, just held me.

What would I do, if Jake died? How would I deal with it? I clung on, letting emotion wash through me. Anger. Pain. Hurt. Agony.

She could have said, *it'll be okay,* like I'd said to Mom, but we didn't know that. I knew the truth—there were no guarantees. I'd have been angry with her if she'd said it. I just needed her to be silent and hold me, and that was all she did.

I didn't know how long it took before the pain ebbed enough for me to let her go, but I felt better—stronger. I was ready to go back in and be the stone pillar Mom, Robin and Dillon needed.

"Do you want to go back?" she whispered into the air between us. There was no judgment, or pity, or anything to annoy me, only support.

"Yeah." God, I couldn't believe this was Portia. Arrogant, belligerent, upper-class, Portia, who I'd had a drunken fondle with on New Year's Eve, just 'cause I fancied the look of her. Now... *now...* This girl was the sun to me.

"Come on." She took my hand and pulled me back toward the

hospital entrance.

The hospital seemed bright, after being outside in the dark.

I hadn't wanted her to tell me everything was gonna be alright, but as we walked through the corridors, I felt it and said it to myself over and over.

Her blue eyes looked at me as we waited for the elevator, asking if I was okay.

"I'm okay. Sorry to drag you in to all this."

"I don't feel dragged, I want to help."

The elevator bell chimed, then the doors slid open. It was empty.

I pulled her into it, leaned back against the metal, and drew her against me. She pressed the button.

Before the doors were even closed, I pressed my mouth down on hers. Her tongue weaved about mine as her fingers gripped my neck. It was complete freedom for a couple of minutes until the bell rang, telling us we were there. My forehead rested against hers as we caught our breath and the doors slid open.

There was cop standing there.

Shit.

She moved away from me. But I gripped her hand and kept her close.

"Justin Preston?"

Play along, keep calm. "Yeah."

Chapter Eleven

I was sitting in a side room facing the cop who'd played welcoming committee outside the elevator. They'd taken the room over to begin an investigation. There was another cop in the corner.

"And you're sure you don't know the names of any of the guys you say you saw in the stairwell." They'd asked me the same question four times.

"Yes." And I was fighting to keep the anger and annoyance out of my voice. It was like they thought I was caught up in it. Like I'd stabbed my own brother.

"And you have *never*, been involved with any gang?" Third time for that question. They were just asking them in a different order, like they thought they'd catch me out, and I'd say, yes.

"The answer is no. Never. Ever. I'm not into any of that. I bring up my brothers, and I'm bringing them up to avoid that crap. They aren't gonna avoid it if I was in a gang. I don't know how someone got their claws into Jake, and I haven't asked him 'cause he's been in surgery…" I was tired. They'd been on at me for an hour, and I had nothing to tell them.

The cop in front of me had been leaning forward with his elbows on his knees, while the other one scribbled down stuff. He leaned back now. His eyes staring at me as if silence was going to break me and make me admit I'd done it.

I stared him out, but tried to keep my expression from getting angry. Just let him see, *I had nothing to say.*

"Well, I guess you can go back to your mother and your girl, but send your brother, Robin, in here."

Cool. Robin was in no state to handle this. But there was no choice. He'd have to deal with it. I just hoped he remembered everything I'd taught him about handling cops. Stay calm and say as little as you have to, otherwise they wrapped your own words up against you.

"Thanks." I nodded at the guy as I stood, feeling the heaviness of exhaustion in my limbs. It must be nearly two a.m.

Apparently, when we'd first come to the hospital, they'd been down at the site of the incident, gathering evidence there. I'd been told that like it was supposed to put the shit up me because I'd think they'd discovered evidence against me.

Before I went out the door, I looked at them both. "Robin is nothing to do with this either. But once you've worked that out, I'd be grateful if you focus on finding the mother-fuckers who are…"

I walked out before they could answer, but the light I'd caught in their eyes before I looked away suggested they might finally believe me.

Robin was sitting next to Mom in the alcove. I couldn't see Portia, but when I reached it, I discovered her lying across the opposite seats, her legs curled up on them and her head pillowed on her coat as she slept. Robin had been watching her, but now he looked at me, his eyes full of questions—and fear.

"They want to talk to you."

He stood. His hand shook as it lifted to rub over his hair.

"You haven't done anything wrong. You've got nothing to worry about. You weren't involved. Just tell them the truth… You'll be okay." I glanced at Mom, who was looking nervous too. She'd had enough run-ins with the cops over Dad, but for different reasons— he had been guilty of gang attacks, thefts and domestic violence.

"Mom, why don't you go in with him? They'd probably let you.

109

They wouldn't let me. They'd think I was in there to threaten him into silence or somethin'. I'll come and get you out if there's any news on Jake."

She stood up and nodded. She knew Robin wasn't ready to face this. Not that she was either. But what else could she do? I looked down at Portia again, suddenly realizing Dillon wasn't there. "Where's—" I didn't get the rest out before Robin pointed to a door at the back of the alcove.

"He's in there, there's a room with two beds for families to stay over. He couldn't stay awake anymore. Portia could have gone in there with him, but she wanted to wait for you. She didn't succeed though."

I sat in the chair Robin vacated as he and Mom walked up the corridor. Portia was well and truly out-of-office, lying still and breathing quietly, looking vulnerable and beautiful—like an angel—in her short burgundy dress, with her stocking clad, slender legs curled up on the seats.

Her high-heeled shoes stood on the floor beneath the chair her head lay on.

I stood up. There was a coffee machine in the corner, I fed a couple of dollars into it and waited while it whirred, producing a cup, and then dispensed the coffee. I sat back down gripping the hot cup. My free hand lifted to my hair, then ran over my face as a wave of tiredness hit me. I wanted to be curled up behind Portia, spooning in her bed.

I sipped the coffee, then rested it on the arm of the chair and tipped my head back against the wall behind me, shutting my eyes.

I was jolted awake by a high-pitched scream. Cold coffee spilt on my leg as I sat forward. Shit. Dillon. I put the coffee down as the door handle of the room he was in rattled like mad, he was trying so hard to get out he couldn't. Portia sat up as I moved, her eyes blinking. She looked startled.

I turned the handle all the way around. It must be slipping through his fingers on the other side. He screamed. When the door opened he was in full on panic.

He had bad dreams; always had done.

"It's okay bro." As I leaned down he flew at me, sobbing his little heart out. I picked him up. His arms slipped about my neck and his legs wrapped about my waist.

"Justin." He said my name as if I was his favorite superhero—Spiderman.

I rubbed his head and pressed it to my shoulder. "It's okay." His tears were wet on my neck.

"I dreamed Jake was bad, and there was blood everywhere."

My hand stilled on his head. It was stupid, because I'd known that for hours, but right then it hit me. That was what had happened. Jake was bad.

Ice ran through me chilling my whole body. "He is bad," I said quietly. "But the doctors are taking care of him. He's gonna be okay." I had to believe it, because my heart and brain couldn't cope with it any other way.

Portia gave me a closed lip smile, before mouthing. "You okay?"

Nodding, I slipped my free hand into my pocket to pull out more change. "Here. Would you get us coffees?" I threw a look at the one I'd put down. "That's cold." She stood up and took the money from me.

I sat down with Dillon straddling my waist still. His face carried on pressing into my neck as I rubbed his back.

"There's chocolate…" Portia offered. "Do you want a cup of chocolate, Dillon?"

He glanced at her and nodded, then went back into hiding. This was the way he was after a bad dream. It wasn't just about Jake—the two of us had our routine of dealing with his dreams when Mom was out. "Take breaths," I whispered to his ear.

As he breathed more deeply, it made the hairs on the back of my neck tickle. My next words were always, "It's just a dream…" But this time it wasn't just a dream…

He lifted his head and his brown eyes looked into mine. "Is

111

Jake gonna die?"

Shit. "No, Dillon." And now I'd promised something I couldn't come through on. I had no control over it.

Portia put our drinks down on the table. I smiled at her. "Thanks. You don't have to stay if you don't want."

"I do want." She turned back to get a drink for herself.

"What time is it?"

She looked at her watch. "Just after three."

They'd been quizzing Robin for an hour.

Dillon's cheek pressed harder against my shoulder, seeking comfort and security.

"Do you want me to read you a story?" He must still be tired, and he always fell asleep on me after he'd had a night-terror, it was part of our routine, letting him know there was someone in his life he could lean on.

"Yeah." His breath brushed my neck again. I looked at Portia. She was just lifting her drink out of the machine. She set it down and went to the box some nurse must have brought in for him.

"A Roald Dahl," Portia said, smiling at Dillon and picking it up. "Fantastic Mr. Fox?" Dillon nodded against my shoulder, having turned his head to watch her.

She sat next to me, opened the book and started reading. Dillon stayed tucked in against me, listening as I worked my tie loose. When I slid it off, I gave it to Portia. "Put it in my jacket pocket." My jacket was on the seat next to her. She kept reading as she did.

I could feel Dillon's body relaxing as she carried on, her voice was like a lullaby, soft and musical.

He fell asleep.

She was watching him, but she read a few more lines.

When she closed the book, she looked at me. "Do you want your coffee?"

I nodded, she got it for me.

"What did the cops say?"

"Nothing, apart from treating me like I'm the criminal."

Her lips twisted sideways. "That's shit."

"You're telling me, and now Robin is in there getting the same grilling, he's in there with Mom. The shitheads."

"But let's hope those shitheads are going to find the people who did this to Jake."

I gave her a grudging smile. "Yeah."

We sat in silence then, letting Dillon sleep, but after we finished drinking the coffee, Portia gripped my hand, and we both rested our heads back against the wall.

"Justin." The next thing I knew Mom was waking me up by gripping my knee. My eyelids flickered open. "Justin." My gaze clung to hers. She looked worried. "They've said we can go and see Jake, but only two of us at a time. I'm taking Robin in first."

He was okay...

Relief, bewilderment, grief... So many strange emotions I hadn't known with this much intensity before fought a war for precedency inside me.

Then suddenly everything that had been happening slipped back into my head. "How did it go with the cops?"

"Question after question, but I think they're satisfied this isn't because of anything you or Robin have done. I think they thought it was some revenge attack. They've spoken to Jake now too, they insisted on going in there before us. I hope it hasn't made him worse."

"The doctors wouldn't have let them go in if they thought it was a risk, Mom."

I looked at Robin. He was still shaky, and obviously desperate to see Jake.

I smiled. He smiled back. He'd grown up good. But now there was Jake... and Dillon. "Robin, fetch me when you're ready to come out."

"Okay."

They turned away.

Portia was awake and watching. "You okay?" she squeezed my

113

hand.

"Yeah." But tears burned my eyes. This time they were tears of relief. I looked up at the ceiling. Surely this meant Jake was gonna be okay.

But what next? None of us could go back to the apartment. It wasn't safe. If the guys who'd stabbed Jake knew the cops were involved, they'd be smashing our door in within hours—and they wouldn't give a shit who was in there. Dillon... Mom...

I spoke to the air above me. "We can't go home, you know? I can't take them back. It's too dangerous. I don't know what we're gonna do."

"That stinks..." she whispered, keeping her voice down because of Dillon sleeping.

I looked at her. "It double stinks." She laughed quietly.

"You're a saint. You know that," she answered once she'd sobered.

"A saint? I think you know that isn't true, Portia."

"It is where your brothers are concerned. I love the way you look out for them."

"Yeah, well I failed with Jake."

"You didn't fail, the boy who stabbed him is the failure..."

When I looked at her I saw something catch in her eyes. "If you get out of that area..." She broke the sentence like she didn't know quite what to say, but she finished. "Sometimes good things come from bad."

I raised an eyebrow at her. Some stupid notion was spinning in her head, I could see it. Dillon started waking up. "You okay, buddy?"

He stretched. His brown eyes looked liquid and sleepy. "How's Jake?"

"Awake, Dillon, and okay. Mom and Robin are with him. We can go in, in a minute, they'll only let two of us in at a time. Do you need the restroom?"

He nodded.

"Come on then, let's go."

114

He climbed off me. I got up and smiled at Portia, before letting him pull me down the corridor.

Portia

I was hungry. I thought they must be too. I decided to go down to the restaurant. I asked a nurse to say to Justin that I'd gone to find us food.

The choice was yoghurts and breakfast bars, or cookies, it was six a.m and they hadn't started serving anything cooked.

An idea had kicked off in my head upstairs, and it just kept spinning as I looked at what there was to eat.

It was a huge idea. But it could solve a lot of things...

I picked up a handful of the breakfast bars, paid for them and went back upstairs. Justin was in the alcove, sitting with Dillon, his hand on top of Dillon's head, as Dillon stood in front of him talking.

I offered Justin a cereal bar. He took it. "Thanks." What was going on between us had hit a whole other platform.

I offered Dillon one. He took it with a mumbled, "Thank you."

Justin and I had a ton of stuff to say to each other, it was in the atmosphere, but neither of us said it because Dillon was there. We ate the breakfast bars, leaving him to talk.

When Justin's brother, Robin, came along the corridor, he looked emotional and as if all he wanted to do was hug Justin.

I needed to go. Robin wouldn't want to be upset in front of me. I was intruding... This wasn't my family.

Yet... there was that idea crowding into my head again.

I stood up and looked at Justin. "You'll want to go in and see Jake. I'll go, leave you to it. Call me later if you want me to come back."

He stood and gripped my arm as Dillon rushed over to Robin. "You don't have to go, Portia." His gaze was tender with emotion.

Yeah, our relationship had hit a whole other universe; there was way more depth in his eyes.

"I know, but Robin wants to confide in you. Call me if you need me. You've got your family here so you'll be okay. I'll go crash at home for a bit. If you need me to get anything let me know—"

"You don't need to throw your money 'round. It won't fix everything, Portia, and I don't want it." His gaze had shuttered the instant I'd said *get*.

Shit… Now I didn't know what to do. That idea in my head had been growing roots and my heart had been saying—*do it*. I nodded… "I know. I was being nice."

He leaned down and kissed me, a firm press of his lips on mine, then he kissed my forehead too. "Sorry. I'll call you later."

"Yeah. Okay." My heart ached, his anger had hurt, but I knew he must have hated taking my money for Jake's treatment.

Then he said, "Thanks." The small word spoken with a huge weight of meaning, it wasn't a small thing for him to say.

"Welcome." I smiled, before turning and then walking away, my heart pounding.

I was just going to do it.

Chapter Twelve

Justin

There were machines all around Jake, and a whole bank of tubes coming out of a thing by his neck that seemed to go into his main artery. Then there were monitor pads on his chest, and a thing clipped on is finger, and a needle connecting a drip into his arm dripping blood from a packet hanging from a thing beside the bed. He looked a mess. My heart hurt.

His head turned to me. He was lying on his back, with a white sheet covering his hips and legs, and there was a huge white pad taped to his torso; blood had seeped through it at the middle and to one side. Then there was a vicious looking wound running up from his belly to his chest, it looked like a zipper. They'd cut him open and then stapled him back up and his skin, that looked pale gray not brown, was stained with a dark yellowy liquid. Iodine.

This was my little brother.

Mom sat in a chair on the other side of the bed. The monitor next to her bleeped a steady pattern and sent various wavy lines across its screen.

Jake was still looking at me. "You okay?" I said quietly.

Stupid question. He was lying in a hospital, cut open and pierced to pieces by needles, having nearly died. But he nodded. Only a tiny movement. Then his eyes turned all shiny. He'd hate crying in front of me but even more so in front of Mom.

I looked at her. "Dillon will want to come in, if they'll let him. Why don't you ask?"

When she went out I gripped Jake's hand, holding it hard. His lips twitched, like some thought passed through his head that stirred his emotion.

He'd probably thought I'd shout at him.

It was too late for that.

"How did you get on with the cops?"

"Okay." He breathed from a dry throat.

I looked over my shoulder and saw a beaker thing. "Can you have water? Do you want some?"

His eyes showed gratitude. "Yeah."

After I'd got it, I supported his head while he drank some.

When I'd put it back, I dragged the other chair in the room up to the bed and sat down.

I gripped his hand again. I felt like he needed the contact— but I wanted contact too. To know he was really here—solid and breathing. "Did you know the guy who stabbed you?"

"Yeah."

"Did you tell the cops?"

"Yeah." He looked at me. He knew what that meant. There was no way we could go back to the apartment. His eyes clouded with concern...

"You don't have to tell me how you got caught up with them, Jake. It's too late to make a difference."

"Sorry."

I gripped his hand harder. "You're alive, and you've got out."

"A guy in my class at school kept talking to me..." He wanted to tell, "I dodged out of school with them just once, but they smashed this guy's car up, and... Justin..."

"It's okay, Jake, it's done." I put my hand on his shoulder. The memories were killing him. He'd been trapped and terrified— caught in a web of lies. That was how the gangs worked—they

118

didn't give you a choice.

He nodded, the tears in his eyes earlier running over. I gripped his hand again.

I couldn't hold him, all his tubes were in the way, but I wanted to. Jake and I had never been close, but now he clung to me, his fingers closing around mine.

He was going to be okay. We just had to find somewhere else to live. But that was not going to be easy.

The door swung open. Jake and I let go of each other as Mom came in with Dillon.

Dillon rushed at Jake but I stopped him. "Be careful, he's a little like patchwork. Be gentle, okay?"

"But you can take my hand." Jake said, lifting his arm.

Dillon did, kneeling on the chair I'd pulled up, saying, "You were covered in blood."

Jake just smiled, trying to ease Dillon's fear.

"I thought you were gonna die. You weren't breathing in the ambulance."

"Sorry. I didn't mean to scare you, bro..." Yeah. Jake was okay. This may be shit, but it had got Jake back on the right path, and hopefully Dillon would remember this and never make the same error. Good things out of bad.

We just had to find somewhere safe to live...

Portia

I slept when I got home, for an hour or so. But my idea was spinning through my head along with images of Justin's family.

As soon as I got up I opened my laptop and started hunting. I found ten properties in Queens. Apartments. I picked up my cell and called the real estate agents. Half the places were wiped out straight away, the people in them weren't ready to move, and I needed somewhere empty. Two more of the properties, the people were caught up in sales chains—they'd take too long. I wanted something quick and easy.

119

I ended up with three possibilities, all three bedroom apartments. I didn't want to buy something too big. One was on the ground floor in a converted house with a yard. Another was a new build. All three were empty. Perfect. I made appointments to go see them straight away, showered quickly and dressed.

My cell rang on the way to the second agent. Justin's image flashed up on my screen as I pulled my cell out of my pocket, him naked to the waist sitting on my bed, giving me a devilish smile right before he pounced on me. I touched the answer icon, praying it was good news. "Hey."

"Hey, baby." He sounded breathless. "Jake's okay, they're keeping him in ICU a little longer, but he's talking and drinking, and he seems good. The cops have already picked up the guy he said stabbed him—"

"But the others are still free..."

"Yeah."

And that's why I was doing what I was doing.

"We're going to crash in the room here for a night, 'til we can work things out."

Shit, I didn't want to tell him over the cell. "Well, you could bring Robin and Dillon to mine, but it would be floor space only. I'm willing to pay for a hotel for your mom."

"No way, Portia. I have some money saved. Leave it to me. I'll sort out a room for us somewhere tomorrow."

But they couldn't live in a cheap hotel, or a single room like mine, for more than a stopover, and they wouldn't be able to afford much else.

"Okay." There was no point in arguing over it on the cell.

I liked the place on the ground floor with the yard but it didn't seem so secure. Their place would need a security system and the new build had one. It had been empty for a few months, as the property market had slowed, so I hoped I'd get a deal on it.

I turned to the guy and made an offer, and he rang the company who were selling it. He eventually gave up acting go between and just handed me the cell as I haggled to get a better price.

I headed back to the hospital at four p.m., having done the deal, signed a deposit agreement, and called Dad's solicitor to get the purchase agreements moving.

Of course Dad's solicitor rang Dad. I got a text when I got off the subway. 'I hear you're buying property. That's good, Portia. Wise. Well done.'

Like I cared what he thought. Neither of them had texted to ask if Justin's brother was okay, or even to say they were sad I'd had to go. I shoved them out of my mind.

"Justin." Dillon was sitting on Justin's thigh, playing a game on Justin's cell.

Justin had such a big brother look. At work, he'd always just been the office joker, laid back. He acted like he didn't have a care in the world. But work was probably where he escaped responsibilities because in reality he was a twenty-two-year-old-going-on-thirty. He had his head screwed on way more than I did. He probably lacked time to enjoy life though. That's what he'd been doing on New Year's Eve.

When he looked at me, a smile cut his face, and he lifted Dillon off his knee as he stood up. "Portia!"

He sounded pleased to see me.

I wondered if the same feeling caught like the pain of a sharp stitch in his chest as it did in mine.

I smiled. Robin was opposite them. He looked better today, less shocked, but still worried. "Hey," I said as he looked up.

"Hey," he answered as Dillon moved over to him, still holding Justin's cell. Robin looked at his little brother as Justin's palms cupped my face, then his lips came down on mine.

I lifted my arms to his shoulders, and his came around me, holding me tight for a few minutes, before ending the pressure of his lips with a sweep of his tongue into my mouth. It said—*I wish I could just be with you, and I didn't have this worry.*

He gripped my waist as I met his gaze. "Where's your mom?"

"With Jake, the doctors are in there."

"Can we go somewhere and talk?"

His eyebrows lifted. "Yeah, if you want…" His tone said, *why?*

I tilted my smile, *wait*.

He looked at Robin. "Hey, bro, keep an eye on Dillon." Robin glanced up and nodded, then looked embarrassed when he caught my gaze.

Justin gripped my hand. "Come on."

We went down to the restaurant to get a coffee, and took a table in the farthest corner. He put two lumps of sugar in his cup, not looking at me as he said, "Go on then, what?"

There was a pitch to his voice that implied he couldn't possibly be interested in my chatter—he was teasing, not blatantly but subtly, just like he would at work. It touched my heart like fingers dipping in a pool.

I smiled, glad that his anxiety had lifted that much. Then I breathed, "Justin, I… I bought an apartment."

His eyes opened wider.

I turned to my purse and searched out the details, then slid them over the table. He looked down.

"I thought. Well… I can rent it out, and your mum could—"

His hand lifted. "No. No way. You bought an apartment for us—"

"I have two million dollars that came from my trust fund." I didn't want him to argue. "I can afford it. Easily. I'd need to rent to someone, so I can let your mum have it for the same rent she paid where you were. It's in Queens."

"In this area of Queens it should be fricking triple. You can't do this, and she won't want it." His brow furrowed. "You can't fix people and things with money, Portia. We don't fucking want you to."

I gripped his hand holding him down when he would have stood and walked off. "Don't you think I know that? Why do you think I haven't touched the money for a year? I didn't want it either. But it's sitting there, doing nothing, and your family needs somewhere—it's an investment anyway. I'll make better interest on it than I do in the bank. It's not a loss on my part, not completely a gift, if you take it—"

He pulled his hand free standing. "We aren't gonna take it." Then he turned away.

I followed, leaving my untouched coffee. "Justin!"

He looked back. "I don't want your pity. I'm not your charity case. Back off, Portia."

That hit. It hurt. Maybe I'd damaged his pride, but there was no need to turn around and punch me verbally.

I stopped walking and let him go. He was angry, and I'd learned after the coffee shop thing, Justin could stay angry for an age. I was going to buy the apartment anyway and maybe, given time, he'd cool down and realize it was the best idea.

Then he'd have to convince his mum though…

I guessed that was going to be harder.

I decided to leave. If he didn't want me here… He had enough going on.

My mood descended to basement level as I left the hospital, and even lower as I sat on the subway. I was angry with him too. He could be a jackass. Stubborn idiot.

When I got off the subway car, I got a text. 'I'm sorry I got angry. The answer's still no. But you didn't have to leave.'

'Well you didn't seem like you wanted me there. How's Jake?'

There was a pause before the reply came back. ':-) Jake's good, they're keeping him in ICU still tonight, just to be safe, but they're hoping to move him out of here tomorrow, as long as he doesn't go downhill tonight.'

'You're okay?'

'Yeah.'

'Look out for yourself as well as the others.'

'Okay.'

When I got to my place, I slipped my cell into my pocket and used my key. My cell vibrated when I walked upstairs, ringing out, *Counting Stars*. I didn't answer it. I pulled my hat off, clutching it as I climbed. I felt miserable. I missed Justin but I needed to recoup for a little while.

My laptop was left open on the bed where I'd been looking at apartments.

I'd thought it a brilliant idea. He didn't.

I stripped my coat off and then dropped on the bed and looked at my cell.

'Missing the fuck out of you.'

'So romantic.'

';D you should've answered my call. I wanted to hear your voice.'

'You can hear it tomorrow. Take care, Justin.'

'Are you gonna come back tomorrow?'

'Maybe.'

'Come back in the morning.' Sunday was the last day I'd be able to spend all day with him. I wondered if Justin would go into work on Monday…

'You want me there then?'

'Course I do.'

'Okay.'

':D X'

The guy was back peddling fast, trying to be nice. I wasn't really in the mood for it right now. The shock of Jake had hit me. I'd been busy doing exactly what Justin had accused me of doing, trying to fix everything, and now he'd stopped me, there was nothing to fill the hole but emotion. Tears streaked down my cheeks. I wiped them away.

Justin texted. I shut my cell off.

It wasn't just the stuff going on with Jake, it was stuff with my parents too. I mean I'd spent a whole year avoiding feeling any of this. But now it hit me like a tidal wave. I curled up on my bed and cried.

Chapter Thirteen

Portia

The buzzer for the downstairs door woke me. Heavy limbed and half asleep, I got up. It buzzed again. God, who was that? No one came here. Maybe someone had ordered pizza and they were just pressing random numbers. I looked at the alarm clock. The red numbers glowed out nine o'clock in the shadow of the moonlight.

Rubbing my eyes, that were puffy and sore from crying, I went over and pressed the buzzer. "Hello."

"Hey, Portia, sorry, babe. I've come to grovel."

"Justin!" I pressed the button to let him in, then I ran out of the room and hurtled down the stairs. I hit him on the second landing, literally flying into him and wrapping my arms around his neck. He caught me hard, toppling back against the wall.

"Sorry, babe," he said to my ear as I started sobbing on his shoulder like an idiot.

"It's not you." I pulled away wiping my eyes, "It's Jake and Mum and Dad. And… life… I've just hit a shit day."

His fingers brushed over my cheek. "And I didn't help. It was stupid getting angry at you. It didn't matter. You were being nice."

I gripped his hand and pulled him upstairs. "I was being awesome! You just don't see it." I looked back at him. "But anyway, I don't want to talk about that. Come on." I pulled him on. "Is

125

your Mom okay? Will they be okay with you gone?"

"They'll be fine. Jake's doing good, they are gonna move him out of ICU as soon as they can. Robin's there. I needed to see you."

I turned and wrapped my arms 'round his neck again. "I needed to see you too."

He was smiling when I let him go, and we started back up the stairs again.

In my room, once he'd taken off his coat, I gripped both his hands. "Do you want to talk?" He was still wearing the shirt and pants he'd worn to the restaurant.

"Not if we're sorted and you forgive me, I'd rather do... other stuff." His eyes caught the moonlight and shone. "Unless *you* wanna talk..."

My answer was a kiss. We both just needed sex.

His tongue pressed into my mouth and his hands gripped my thighs, then he lifted me and dropped me back on the bed, coming over the top of me instantly.

I gripped his shirt as he flicked the buttons on my jeans free. Then he leaned back, kneeling, so I could pull his shirt off.

He grinned at me as I sat up and started sliding off my jeans and panties. He undid his pants.

Our clothes ended up in a growing pile on the floor but I still had my bra and top on.

One of his knees landed between my parted thighs, and he leaned over to sort that out.

My heart pounded and my temperature soared.

I got wetter just at the thought of him.

My top and bra were thrown to the floor, then he reached to the bedside drawer for a condom.

Within seconds the guy was on top of me and in me.

This was not just sex. It was escape, letting go, running from the emotion we'd been lacerated by for the past twenty-four hours. He pressed into me driving hard, and I gripped his head, bracing him with my fingers as his clawed in the bedcovers, holding his

126

body weight while his hips worked; dropping with a sudden thrust that had my body jolting. Sparks of sensation flew through my nerves. The guy drove me nuts, while I fought to keep hold of reality—and a hold of him.

He was slipping into madness, he looked so determined, and his eyes were focused but glazed, he wasn't really seeing.

My vision got hazy and my body arched, pushing hard back in the two minutes before I came. My fingers fell to his shoulders. I couldn't grip anymore, he was driving me mad too.

"Justin…"

"Don't talk."

I shut my eyes, giving in to it, riding his storm. The guy had a crazy passionate streak.

"Uhhh."

I was panting, and he kept pounding like a piston thrust and…

"Justin." I closed my eyes tighter and rode the wave of ecstasy that swept in, washing my body clean of bad feelings. He didn't stop and I came again instantly. And again. I knew this wasn't for me but for him. He was gaining control of life—by gaining control of me. I didn't give a fuck. I'd let him take control when his taking was like this. Daniel could never have done this.

I clung to Justin's biceps, not knowing what else to do except hang on, and I held my body steady against his thrusts as orgasm crashed in over orgasm. Shit. Oh my God.

He was growling by the end of it, sweating hard and powering into me even harder. Then he came, and he yelled.

As I felt his orgasm, another hit me.

His forehead dropped to mine—he had it hard, and his chest filled with air, pressing against my breasts.

Guilt washed in, in the aftermath, I'd just had the best sex I'd ever had—because his brother was in an intensive care room.

When he got his breath back, he pulled away, withdrawing, and sitting back on his haunches.

I lifted to my elbows.

"Sorry." His voice was deep.

I sat up and put my arms about his middle, holding tight, my legs still either side of him. "You don't have to be sorry. Do you feel better?"

His hand ran over my hair. "I feel like shit. I feel like I should have been able to stop it happening, I feel... fucked up..."

I didn't answer. There wasn't an answer. He knew he wasn't really fucked up, or at fault. He just needed holding.

A tear dropped on my hair. I still didn't move, and then his body started jerking as his lungs pulled in air and he sobbed and held me.

We stayed like that for ages, even after he'd stopped crying and was silent.

When he let me go he didn't say anything, but moved off the bed and discarded the condom, then came back as I lay down, and lay down next to me, his arms opening so I could snuggle against him. I fell asleep.

Justin

I woke at four a.m. Portia was still asleep. I wanted to get back to the hospital. I needed to be back there. Jake was probably fine, and Mom, Robin and Dillon but... Just, but... I needed to be back there. I'd escaped. I'd got the shit that was eating me up out, and I'd conquered the burning need I'd had for Portia. Now I just needed to go back and be big brother again.

I had a shower to wake myself up, using her shampoo and soap. Then I got dressed. My shirt stunk. I'd been wearing it for two days, but I didn't have anything else to wear.

I was slipping my boots on, sitting on the edge of the bed when Portia woke up.

"You okay?" Her voice was husky.

I looked back. There was a line of moonlight across her middle, falling over the comforter, outlining her body as she sat up. Her hand pushed back her hair. "Yeah. I'm gonna go back to the

128

hospital, Portia."

"Do you want me to come?"

"Only if you want to, you don't have to." But actually I'd like it. "Yeah."

She shifted instantly, getting up and hurrying around in order to get dressed.

I leaned back on the bed waiting. She was ready in fifteen minutes, her hair brushed and braided, her jeans on, and a loose sweater covering the top she'd put on. She tossed me my jacket, then pulled on hers. We'd be at the hospital for about quarter past five. Mum and the boys would probably be asleep, and we wouldn't be allowed to disturb Jake. Even so, I just had to be there.

The woman on reception nodded at us, so did a nurse who was sitting at the desk leading into the ICU ward. I gripped Portia's hand tighter.

But when we rounded the corner of the corridor, leading to the alcove where we'd spent the last two days, I saw something weird.

There was guy at the end of it. A black guy. I was black and I shouldn't judge *but*... It didn't feel right. His hand was behind his back, as if he gripped something, hiding it; it was something tucked into his pants beneath his leather jacket.

My fingers clasped Portia's tighter as I followed.

He can't have heard us, he didn't turn 'round, just kept walking, with a street swagger.

He had an attitude. I could feel it radiating from him. He wasn't young. He looked late twenties. But everything about him made my skin itch.

This wasn't right.

He kept walking.

I kept walking, lifting a finger to my lips to silence Portia as we walked past the alcove. *Shit. This was not right.*

He still had his hand at the back of his pants and was striding along in a chilled out pace, but he didn't look chilled. He looked nervous. His muscles moved stiffly.

I kept on walking, pulling Portia with me.

Then the mother-fucker turned toward the door Jake lay behind. Fricking... He didn't look back at us even then, and I knew why, because he was hiding his face from the hospital's security cameras and trying to make out like it was perfectly normal for him to stroll into Jake's room. There was no way he was a doctor, and no way was he a plain clothes cop.

I looked back at Portia, letting her fingers go. "Go for help, that's Jake's room and that isn't right."

Her mouth opened in shock, but it only took her a second to react before turning and running back toward the nurses' desk. I carried on.

It never occurred to me to think of myself—to not run toward Jake's room. Not for an instant. I never even slowed at the door, just shoved it open.

The mother-fucker!

The guy was leaning over Jake, pressing the barrel of a gun into Jake's forehead. Jakes eyes turned to me, full of terror. Jake never looked to me for help—never—he'd hated me taking Dad's place. He'd even blamed me for Dad leaving. But now... Now he looked at me like he was drowning in the sea, and I was the only boat in sight. I could think of nothing to do but go at the guy. Portia had all the talk. I just had my fists. I charged at him, shouting.

A loud sharp bang resonated in the air around me as I powered into him and the gun went off; deafening me for an instant and leaving my ears ringing.

The guy fell backwards and I came down on top of him. His head hit the hard floor-tiles and rebounded. The force drove the air from his lungs. Pulling back on to my knees, I thrust my fist at his jaw. Sirens screamed outside the hospital and Jake's machine was going off, sending out a distress call.

I struck the guy's jaw again, my mind screening out the noise. I gripped his collar pulling him up, his head lolled back, but I still hit him one more time. Then someone was in the room, in scrubs, hauling me off and a guy pinned my arms behind me, while voices spoke to Jake, moving about the bed.

Shit.

Consciousness crowded back in on me as the room filled up.

The guy had had a gun pointed at Jake.

Jake was dead. I'd heard the gun fire. I couldn't hear him; all I could hear was his machine screaming that he'd flat-lined.

Shit.

The guy who'd pulled me up was still gripping both my arms behind my back. "Let me go! Let me go! He's my brother!" The guy's grip eased and I turned. "Jake!" I expected to see his brains blown out... I expected... I feared...

He was looking at me, his eyes wide, dark orbs with the lights in the room still out.

I shut my eyes. *Thank you God. Whatever God you really are. If you're there... Thanks.*

"Justin..." He said weakly, I opened my eyes. Jake was looking at the guy who held me. "He is my brother."

The guy let me go and I went to Jake and gripped his hand. "What the fuck, Jake?"

"He uses the gang to move drugs. He was checking I hadn't told the cops."

"Jake..."

"I'm sorry."

I gripped his hand. "It's okay. You're out of it now, and you were trying to get out of it."

Tears slipped from his eyes. "I messed up."

"You did. But you can put it right now."

And shit, I'd have to put it right too; there was no choice anymore.

There was a load of noise outside. People. Someone stopped the sound Jake's machine was making. Then I saw the little sticky pad attached to a cable, dangling by the bed. He'd pulled his heart monitor off, to make out he'd flat-lined, to get someone in here.

131

I pressed his shoulder again and a tear ran from his eye. I wiped it away.

"It's gonna be okay." I said as three cops pushed through the door.

The burly medics in the room moved the guy on the floor so the cops could cuff him. There would be more painful interviews now.

"I better go see Mom."

Jake nodded. But a cop stopped me before I could get out.

"You're not going anywhere, boy."

"I just wanna tell my mom, he's okay. Then I'll come back."

"We'll tell your mother. You need to speak to us first."

Mom was gonna be left worrying. Portia… The boys…

Portia

I wished they'd let us see Justin. He'd been gone for nearly two hours. Dillon was sitting with me. Robin and Justin's Mom were too anxious to entertain him. We'd been told some guy had taken a gun into Jake's room, that Jake wasn't injured and that Justin wasn't injured, but nothing else.

My heart pounded out a rhythm as if I was standing against a base speaker and it reverberated through me. I could feel my heartbeat in my fingertips. I turned another page of the book Dillon was reading to me.

I'd lost patience with waiting. Come on, let him go. He must be so tired.

I thought of Jake too. Lying in that bed all alone, he'd had a shock. He probably wanted to see his mum.

Come on.

I focused back on Dillon. At least I was helping in some small way. Justin's mum smiled at me, she'd kept smiling. I smiled back.

When Justin finally walked down the hall ten minutes later, his fingers were rubbing his forehead, as if he had a headache, and his knuckles were split open.

Dillon jumped up and rushed toward him, hugging him around

the waist when he got there. Justin's hand came down on Dillon's shoulder and squeezed it.

His mum and Robin stood, and went to meet him in the hall. I stayed back.

"What happened?" his mum asked.

"A guy was using the gang Jake got caught up in to deliver drugs. He didn't want Jake telling. He thought he'd scare him into silence. Unfortunately for him, I caught him doing it… He's been arrested. It means that Jake's gonna have to go to court twice though. Have you seen him?"

Mrs. Preston shook her head.

"We better go see him." Justin looked at me, his eyes saying sorry. I smiled. I wanted to hold him but he had to see his brother first. I respected that. I respected him.

"Dillon…" Justin looked down. "Be good, stay with Robin, we'll be back in a while. Then you can come in and see Jake."

Dillon sighed, the poor kid was bored of waiting out here, but he turned to Robin.

Justin turned away, his arm bracing his mum's shoulders.

"Why don't we go down to the restaurant or the store or something…" I suggested to Dillon.

Robin looked at me. "Don't leave me on my own up here." He was tired, worried—we all were.

"Then come."

Robin gripped Dillon's hand. I walked on the other side of him. I loved how close these brothers were. I'd built up a ton of respect for Justin's mum too.

"What's between you and Justin?" Robin asked as we walked up the corridor.

I looked at him, and his question echoed in my head. What were we? Boyfriend and girlfriend. Dating. It didn't feel like *just* that, anymore.

"You've hung out here a lot," Robin added, meeting my gaze. His eyes were the same shade as Justin's, same long dark eyelashes.

"Yeah. But we're only dating." As I said it there was an ache in my chest that said that was an utter lie, there was no *only* about it.

Justin

I itched to see Portia. Literally. My hands hurt with a need to touch her. That was how I'd felt last night when I'd raced out of the hospital and headed over to hers. But now it was more than just a sexual itch—it was a soul deep itch. My spirit longed for her.

When I came out of Jake's room, leaving Mom with him, my heart was thumping, like some guy was banging a fist against my ribcage in my chest. But she wasn't there. None of them were.

My heart clenched. God, if Portia had got caught up in my family's shit...

I headed for the nurses' desk at the end of the hall and leaned over it pinning the woman with my gaze. "Where's my family?"

She gave me a placating smile, she knew what we'd gone through this morning. "They're downstairs, probably getting a drink or something... Oh, and we are going to move your brother in about an hour. There's a room available in a ward upstairs."

I nodded, emotion twisting in my belly. *He was gonna be okay.*

I turned away.

My heart pounded. I wanted to know Robin and Dillon were safe... *but her*, I wanted to see Portia most. No girl had come higher than my family before.

My hands clenched into fists then released about a dozen times as I stood in the elevator. The itch in my blood getting stronger.

I followed the signs to the restaurant in the basement level... If they weren't there...

I threw the door wide as I walked in, my eyes scanning the place. They were there. It hurt to look at her. She was leaning toward Robin, and they were laughing, and Dillon was sitting next to Robin playing with something they must have got him in the shop.

Relief flooded my veins followed by an intense flow of need. Something attached me to Portia, something binding. I was well

134

and truly caught now.

I walked over to them. Portia was the first to notice me. She leaned back, when she saw me and her face lit up, no exaggeration, she literally glowed with joy, showing as much relief as I felt, then concern clouded her expression as she stood. "You okay?"

"Okay now," I answered as I hugged her fiercely, lifting her off her feet. Then I put her down and kissed her.

When I let her go Robin was looking away awkwardly, and she was blushing as Dillon stared up at us.

Portia's fingers brushed my cheek and then ran up over my head. I was still holding her waist.

"You really okay?"

"Yeah, honest."

She smiled. "Robin's been dishing some dirt on you."

"Like what?"

Her fingers pressed against my cheek and her smile grew. "He's told me about your ex-girlfriends."

My eyebrows lifted and I looked at Robin. He shrugged. The sneak.

"He said, you've never had a serious thing with anyone. He thinks we're serious."

I laughed. "Nice of *him* to tell you."

Robin's eyebrows lifted at me now. "Well, you don't want to lose this one do you…" Life advice from my seventeen year old brother—crazy.

"Take Dillon upstairs, you can go in and see Jake. Mom's in there. He's okay, tired, and shaken up, but okay. He's learned his lesson."

Robin nodded and Dillon scrambled out of his seat, looking up at me.

"You alright, kid? Jake's gonna be okay. They're moving him out of ICU soon."

"He nodded grinning at me." I caught him in a loose headlock and rubbed his head with my sore knuckles before letting him go. He was laughing when he slipped away and ran off ahead of Robin.

I turned back to Portia.

"You're so good with them," she said.

"You've been pretty good with them too. Thank you. You being around made this easier." Now I knew I had to say something, but the words were sticking in my throat. Pride. But I had common sense too.

"Sit down, Portia, and finish your coffee." My voice came out more serious than I intended, callous probably, but it was due to my inner battle, not her. *Common sense.*

The pleasure in her expression collapsed. She did sit down though.

I rubbed a hand over my face; feeling the pressure, worry and exhaustion of the last forty-eight hours hit me. My hand fell to the table and she gripped it.

"Do you want me to get you a coffee?"

I shook my head. "No the cops got me one." I turned my hand in hers, so our palms touched, that was where our colors collided. Then I looked up at her blue eyes. She was not the girl I'd thought she was months ago, she was all things good.

"I want to accept your offer of the apartment to rent. I'm sorry I got so angry over it. It's a good idea. Sensible. No way can we go back to the Bronx. Mom is going to have to accept it. Your help is kind of like a miracle. Thank you." She knew how much it cut me to say it. I could see the understanding in her eyes—and thank fuck she didn't gloat.

"Okay. Everything's still going through, I didn't call it off. I'd have bought it anyway."

"Well it's not going to be easy convincing Mom. But you were right. As this morning proved, those guys are going to keep looking for Jake, and us. All of us. We need to start again somewhere, and your help means we can."

I looked down out our hands, then up again. "I feel shit about it…"

She smiled gently. "I know."

"And if anything happens between us…"

"We'll deal with it then, Justin, but right now, we can't know the future, but I do know that all I want is you in it. Just you…" Her fingers curled around my hand.

Yeah. "That's how I feel too."

Chapter Fourteen

Justin

Portia laughed throwing my jacket at me. "We're late. If Mr. Rees is in, we're gonna be in a whole pile of shit."

"Well you shouldn't look so sexy when you wake up and I wouldn't want to do you."

"Do me… Romantic."

I smiled at her as I pulled on my jacket. "I'll romance you anytime, baby."

She grimaced at me over her shoulder as she opened the door. "For that, you can cook tonight."

"For that, I will, but I'll blindfold you when you eat it."

"Fuck off with all your kinky shit..."

"You love kinky…"

She gave me an evil eye as she grabbed an umbrella and walked out. Rain was hammering down on the skylight above.

I laughed.

We'd been living together for two months. I'd stayed with Mom and the others for a month after Jake got out of the hospital, making sure they settled. But Mom had changed her shifts now, she only worked when Dillon and Jake were at school, and she walked to and from school with them. They were in new schools; on the far side of Queens, well away from any of the rough areas in the Bronx.

It hadn't really been a decision to move in with Portia; it had just happened. I'd started staying over, and then I'd just never left and moved more and more of my clothes across.

I'd never lived with a girl before, but now that we were a couple, I was with her 24-7. Still, I kept shaking things up with a bit of kinky stuff and silly dates to make sure we didn't get boring. Portia hadn't got with me because I was boring and I didn't want to lose her.

When we got down to the street, we hit the rain. It was pouring down, hard and fast. She opened the umbrella before stepping out and raised it. She was in her in-office mode. It slipped over her when she got dressed in the morning. But her in-office personality was getting left behind more and more. She still looked different at work but she didn't always act different.

"Come under," she said, as I flicked up my hood. *Couple-y.*

"I'm alright."

"You're getting wet."

"I can cope with wet."

She rolled her eyes at me, but then a gust of wind blew the rain sideways right up under her umbrella, catching the thing and trying to pull it from her hand. She squealed. I gripped the handle, my hand over hers and my other hand caught the brim to hold it steady.

See, now I was cowering under an umbrella with her. But the look I got for it was worth it.

The prim perfect Portia was still at her core, the one that had to have everything right because she'd been shouted at too many times for getting things wrong as a kid. She'd hate going into work soaked.

I told her every day that she was perfect to me.

She laughed and stopped walking, her gaze tangling up with mine. Her blue eyes made me forget we were in the middle of a busy street getting in people's way. I let go of the rim of the umbrella as her mouth opened.

"I love you." She said it like it was a discovery.

My other hand loosened from over hers as they gripped the handle of the umbrella.

"I think I've felt it for ages," she whispered, her eyes shining at me. "But just now, the words leaked out of my heart and they were everywhere. I love you, Justin, seriously. I hope we last… You're all I want."

My hands came up with the same tug of emotion she must have felt—it was spewing like a volcano inside me. My palms pressing against her cheek bones, my fingers curved in her hair. "I love you too", I said, right before I kissed her. Love, longing, need… commitment… swayed around inside me.

The rain hit me. The umbrella was gone. I broke the kiss and looked into her eyes, "You're all I want too. *Just you, baby*. Nothing is gonna happen to us…" Her parents could do their best to split us up, they'd been trying. They wouldn't succeed. They only pushed her closer to me, and couple-y wasn't gonna be boring when she was the other half of it—of me.

Whatever trance held us broke as another gust of wind blew, stinging rain into our faces. "Shit, Justin…" She looked away, and my gaze followed to see the umbrella sailing on the wind down the street, causing cars to slam their breaks on, screeching to a halt. Laughing like idiots we both turned and started chasing the thing.

Chapter Fifteen

Justin

My palms were sweating. I wiped them on my pants. I knew for a fact that Portia would not want me to do this. But I had to... I'd been brought up to do things right, and if I was going to do anything right. Then it was going to be this.

Shit. When my hand lifted to knock on the wooden door leading into her dad's office, all my muscles tensed, gripping and trying to stop me from doing this. I ignored the instinct to run and struck the door hard with a single knock.

Then I rolled my shoulders back and let my hands drop, trying to relax. I wanted to look confident. I was not going to let the guy make me feel small.

"Come!" The firm call came from within.

I glanced over at his personal assistant who sat at a desk behind me. She nodded. Like I was Dillon and needed encouragement.

I thought of Portia who would be in the office back in New York. I'd lied to her. I'd even persuaded Keith, the editor, to lie her. I'd asked him to tell me in front of her that he wanted me to go out of town to a photo shoot to make sure they set it up right. Wrong.

I'd caught a plain to California last night to come see her dad. I'd been full of determination then, but now... now it was something a little like cowardice that gripped in my belly.

Shit. I took a deep breath just as the PA's intercom buzzer went. Then Portia's Dad's voice blasted through it. "Is he coming in or not?"

Yeah, he was going in…

My hand gripped the door handle and pushed down, opening it.

My back stiffened as I walked in and then closed the door behind me; trying not to look weak or nervous, and not to turn my back on him—the enemy.

I took another subtle deep breath, before turning fully, facing him directly and looking him in the eyes. Portia had got her eye color from him.

"Justin."

He didn't stand up. He sat behind his big impressive desk, looking one-hundred percent the domineering billionaire with the world at his feet.

My spine stiffened even more as I pulled up to full height, letting the determination that had brought me out here flood my nerves. "Mr. Hemming."

He tapped the end of the fountain pen he had gripped in his hand on the edge of the desk impatiently. "So tell me, to what do I owe this honor?"

I'd met Portia's parents about six or seven times in the months we'd been together. They didn't like me. Every time it had been awkward. They didn't think I was good enough for her. Financially and socially—I wasn't. But none of that mattered because *she* thought I was good enough. We just went. We got on. We laughed together. We connected. She was such a part of my life now that I couldn't define anymore what was mine, and about me, and what was her. We were one thing. Portia and Justin.

I wanted to wipe my palms again but I didn't. I stayed standing, kept my shoulders relaxed and met his glare that said I was nothing but a piece of dirt from the ghetto, who shouldn't be anywhere within a mile of his daughter. "I am gonna ask Portia to marry

142

me. I've come to get your blessing."

He leaned back suddenly like I'd punched him, his fingers gripping the arms of his chair as his eyes widened. Then he recovered, still sitting back, he tilted one eyebrow at me. "And you seriously think I am likely to give it to you?"

"No…"

The sneer playing with his lips had me riled and my anger rocketed.

I leaned on his desk, but I kept my voice down so his Personal Assistant wouldn't hear, but I wanted to get this straight so I shoved my words in his face. "But I'll marry her anyway. I just wanted to do the right thing…" My palms pressed down on the smooth, dark wood, and my fingers splayed wide as I leaned further over. His blue gaze held mine, hard and fixed. "…and I want you to do the right thing too. By her."

I straightened up again, standing and looking down on him. "It isn't her fault you mess around. And it isn't her fault your wife puts up with it. It wasn't her fault she was brought up by strangers, miles away from you. That's your fault. She may act like she doesn't give a shit about you. But that isn't true and I hope you know that."

I left a pause but he didn't speak or nod, or anything.

"Well anyway, I came all the way here to do the right thing and tell you to do the right thing too. You can keep refusing to accept we are together. That's fine, it's your choice…" My hands lifted and gripped the tense muscle at my waist, but I let them fall when I heard Dillon's voice in my head—*you look like a superhero standing like that.*

I'd rehearsed this speech so many times on the way up here, and right now I was hanging on to my nerve with an iron grip, but I was no superhero, just a guy trying to make this idiot see sense.

"If you carry on, you are gonna lose her completely. She wants me. I know that. I know she's gonna say yes and eventually she'll get too pissed off with you sniping and cutting at me to bother seeing you at all. That's fine by me if that's what happens. She'll cope, 'cause she's strong. She proved it to you when she walked out and set up a life in New York.

"But that isn't what she wants. She wants you to be a Dad. Dependable. Reliable—*not* embarrassing. It's up to you. Do what you want. But one day, the two of us are gonna get married and have kids. You can change and give Portia what she deserves from a father, or you can carry on, just as you are, and have nothing to do with our lives and your future grandkids. Up to you…"

I sighed.

"I'm glad my dad's gone. I never want to see him again. If he turned up, or I saw him in a street, I'd walk past him and pretend he wasn't there. Is that what you want Portia to do to you? My dad's a lost cause. Nothing would make him change.

"But you… You're an intelligent man. When the fuck are you going to grow up and start being a father to her? You are better than this…" I threw the last words at him with a pointed finger to enhance them as anger rushed into my voice.

That was it. I was done. I'd said my piece. I'd tried. "You can listen to me or not, up to you. I don't care. Have a nice day, Mr. Hemming"

With that I turned my back and started walking out. I'd done what I had come here to do, now I could go back to Portia and do what I really wanted to do.

As my hand touched the metal door handle. I heard him move, like he was sitting forward. "Justin!"

My hand still on the door, I glanced back, my gaze clashing with the intense blue-gray of his.

"You have my permission."

I turned away again before he could see the smug smile that crept over my lips. "Thank you." I opened the door, without looking back, and walked out.

Portia

144

Justin's fingers gripped my hand harder, they were wrapped right around it, and the pressure of his grip seemed anxious. He was in a weird mood today. He came over really nervous. Justin was always relaxed but he wasn't relaxed today. As he held my hand, his arm didn't hang loosely like it normally would, the tension in his muscles made the grip, and the movement of his arm, feel awkward.

We were walking around Central Park. The sun was out. The day wasn't hot but when you were in the bright sunshine, it heated your skin. It was one of those days when one minute you wanted to strip off your sweater and then the next, when you hit a shaded avenue of trees, the chill caught you and you wanted to put it back on. I'd left mine on for now, just absorbing the heat of the May sunshine into my bones, after such a freezing, hideously harsh winter. This was so nice.

I glanced up at Justin as we walked around the water where there were loads of kids with their Dad's playing with model boats. I guess this was a haunt for broken families, for guys who had their kids to spend a few hours of contact with on a Sunday. "Are you okay, Justin. You seem really tense. Is something wrong?"

His brown gaze came down to me as his head turned, and his broad lips twisted a little, in an expression that confirmed his anxiety. But verbally, he denied it. "Fine. Just enjoying the company and the sunshine."

I'm sure my expression showed some doubt.

"Nothing is wrong with your Mom or the others?"

He'd had to go away on a job for the magazine in the week, he'd been acting odd before that, and even odder since he came back; like he was uncomfortable. If I didn't know any better my battered belief in people would think he was having an affair, the way he'd been acting all secretive and holding back on me since he'd been told about this trip to take part in a shoot for the magazine—and yet, I had heard Kevin ask him to go, so I knew the trip was genuine.

145

I looked ahead again as we came up to the opening of the paved area, where the sculpture of Alice in Wonderland stood.

There were more kids there. I pulled on Justin's hand. To go look at it for a moment.

He let my hand go as we walked over and then rubbed his palm on the backside of his jeans. He was nervous, but he wasn't admitting it, and I didn't know why.

There was a boy, maybe around four or five, gripping the bronze ears of the March Hare and dangling from them like the Hare was a climbing frame. Kids were always climbing all over it. Another little girl sat on one of the mushrooms gripping the doormouse, like she was joining in the tea-party.

I sat down on the bench that ran in a three-quarter circle about the sculpture, caught by a sudden sense of longing and happiness as the girl's mother walked up behind her, touched her shoulder, and leaned over to join in the game. A man came up then and touched the woman's shoulder as another little girl who looked so like the one on the mushroom, but older, ran around to the other side and climbed up the figures to claim a seat on Alice's lap.

Alice in Wonderland.

My fingers gripped the cold bench as Justin sat next to me, resting his elbows on his knees and leaning forward.

I felt like Alice in Wonderland. I'd lost faith in life, in people, love and happy endings. But now I had that back. Justin may have been in a weird mood but I didn't doubt him at all. I knew I could trust him. I believed we'd have our happy ending.

I glanced at him.

His head was down, like he was focusing on something mentally. Maybe it was just something at work stressing him out. I think the shoot he'd been called out to do had been some sort of big deal.

Letting go of the bench, my hand then lifted and settled on the firm muscle of his back. He hadn't even worn a coat, he just had a black cotton T-shirt on but he was warm beneath it. "I love you."

His head turned to look at me, the movement of his muscle

stirring beneath my fingers, and he gave me a broad wide reassuring smile; some thought hovering in the depths of his brown eyes. "I love you, too. Come on, let's go hire a row boat out, seeing as the day's so nice."

I smiled too. "That would be fun."

His fingers wove in between mine and clung a little too aggressively to be normal as we queued, and when I offered to go halves on the boat hire, he discouraged me with a grunt. "No, just let me pay. This is my thing."

"Okay." Something was definitely up if Justin had got snappy.

I'd wait until we were out on The Lake and then I'd probe him carefully, and see if I could pull whatever it was out of him. I guessed he needed to talk it out, and then he'd be okay after…

A guy held the row boat as Justin gripped my hand and I climbed in. Then as I perched on a wooden bench at one end, he got in and occupied the one at the other end.

"Have you rowed before?"

"Yeah, but do not expect perfection…" He threw me a smile, and a glint caught in his eyes, flashing a hint of his usual self.

As the guy pushed us off, Justin gripped the oars firmly, leaning forward and dipping them into The Lake, then with a strong stroke, he leaned back and the boat cut through the water. Little splashes and ripples stirred either side of us.

"I used to row lots. There's a lake in the grounds of my parents' house. I can take over—"

"Maybe after…"

After what?

I didn't say anything, just leaned to one side, dipped my fingertips in the water and enjoyed the sensation of it as he, pretty skillfully, cut us a path out into the middle. He wasn't a bad rower at all. "We'll have to bring Dillon with us and come and do this again."

He smiled.

"He'd love it—"

"Yeah, and he'd be fighting me to have a go on the oars, and crash us into the bank…" He laughed.

He was relaxing now; his gaze was warmer.

I sat up, smiling at him. "This day is perfect isn't it?"

A deep breath pulled into his lungs suddenly, swelling his chest, and the anxiety that had been hovering for hours, maybe days, suddenly flooded his eyes, and stiffened his posture. My gaze left his as he moved, pulling the oars into the boat. What on earth was going on that he was so messed up by it?

Leaving the oars in the brackets, he shifted off the seat and one knee dropped onto the hull of the shallow boat as his other stayed raised, and his hand pulled something out of his jeans pocket.

"Here—"

"Justin, kneeling in a boat is not a good idea," It rocked unsteadily, as his hand lifted, with something gripped in his fingers.

He caught hold of my left hand as I saw the sunlight catch whatever he gripped. It sparkled.

Oh my God.

My gaze lifted to meet his. His brown eyes glowed with love and questions, shining like dark amber. "Yes, it is a perfect day. But what makes it most perfect, Portia, is that I'm with you. I want to be with you forever. I want to marry you. Not in a hurry, just whenever. But I want to make sure I've claimed you now so you know just how I feel and everyone else does too. Will you marry me?"

His eyes burned with emotion. The same emotion gathered inside me in a storm, spinning in excited turmoil.

My hand shook as I clasped his fingers, absorbing the solidity of his grip. He was reliable, my best-friend—everything I'd ever dreamed of. "Yes." There was no doubt in me, but the word came out on a stunned breathless whisper. I swallowed, took a breath and said it more clearly. "Yes. I want to marry you. Oh, Justin…" Tears came in a rush as I let go of his hand and threw my arms around his neck leaning forward. "Thank you…" I sobbed as he laughed and the boat rocked, water slapping at the sides.

148

"Steady." His pitch was deep. "You'll make me drop the ring, and we'd lose it forever if it goes in the Lake."

I sat back, sobbing and wiping tears away, shaking. Now he was relaxed, his muscle loose and his vibe easy as he took up my left hand again.

The touch of his fingers was gently protective as he slid the ring on.

Emotion caught about my heart and squeezed tight, more tears trickling down my cheeks as I looked at it.

The gold was warm, and a beautiful solitaire diamond glinted up at me, sparkling in the bright sunlight.

The pressure of Justin's fingertips lifted my chin, and then his warm, wide lips pressed against mine.

My hand, wearing his ring, came up to the back of his head—I still loved the shape of his head—and I pressed my lips back against his and then opened my mouth. Then I remembered with a flash of an image, doing exactly the same thing in the pool on New Year's Eve, it had been me who'd started this.

My drunk brain had been way more intelligent than I'd thought.

When the kiss broke, his forehead pressed against mine, as we breathed steadily, sharing breaths.

I laughed quietly. "Dad will go nuts you know."

Justin's long narrow fingers embraced the back of my neck and squeezed, in comforting reassurance. "He won't."

Then he leaned back a little smiling.

"I never went on a photo shoot for the magazine. I went to speak to your dad. I asked for his permission to marry you."

My body jolted back, rocking the boat, as he moved on to the opposite bench again.

"No! What did he say?"

"Yes."

"He didn't…"

"He did. Call him."

"You're kidding me…" Even though I answered with disbelief,

I was already searching for my cell.

Justin caught hold of the oars and started rowing, watching me with a smile; it carried happiness and humor. I found out Dad's contact and called his cell. Looking at Justin as it started ringing.

"Hello, Portia." His voice was heavy and deep, but it sounded warm—different.

"Dad." I took a breath and let it slip back out of my lungs. "I'm engaged. To Justin…" As I said the words, there was a grip of wonder inside me. *I was engaged to Justin.* We'd get married, build a life together, have kids. I had a happy ending to hold on to—a fairytale I really believed in.

"I know—" I could hear him smiling. Now that was weird, he hated me being with Justin.

"He said he asked you."

"He did."

"And?"

"And I gave him my agreement. I respect the boy for coming out to California. I guess, you've found a good one after all, Portia…"

I looked at Justin, my eyes trying to express my disbelief. He just smiled.

I wish I knew what he'd said. I wish I'd been there.

"Is it Portia?" Mom sounded like she was near him, "let me talk to her…"

"Congratulations," Dad said, in a firm voice, like he meant it.

"Portia!" Mom sounded breathless and excited. "You have my congratulations too, sweetheart, and you will never guess where we are…"

I smiled at Justin. This was weird. Dad had sounded warm and emotional, Mom really happy and excited—Alice in Wonderland— maybe I had fallen down the white rabbit's hole.

"Where are you?" I answered, hearing the questioning note in my voice, that was not asking that, but asking what is going on…

"We're in Italy, driving along the road by Lake Garda. We are doing an Italian tour. We will be out here for a month, travelling all over. Your father wants to relive our honeymoon—"

What?

"We are going to Venice, and Rome, and Sienna..." She kept talking. Odd feelings overwhelmed me. I'd never heard her sound like this. "But first we're spending a week in the villa we stayed in just after we were married..."

"Is everything okay, Mum?"

"Oh, yes, everything is wonderful..." I had never heard her so enthusiastic. Then the sound was muffled a little, like she had half covered the phone with her hand, and she whispered. "You may thank that boyfriend of yours from me. Since he came down here, it is like your dad has just woken up. We are working on our marriage. We have started seeing a counselor, and we'll carry on after the holiday. I feel so happy, Portia... But I'd better go, we are nearly there, and I need to look out for the sign. Goodbye darling, congratulations. I am going to have to come to New York when you start dress shopping."

"Goodbye, Mum."

"I love you." I couldn't remember the last time she had said that to me, and sounded like she meant it. But that is what it sounded like now. She must have been hurting over Dad's infidelity for years.

I'd been judging her, for how she'd chosen to deal with it. But maybe she hadn't really been dealing with—just ignoring it. Maybe she just hadn't known how to deal with it.

"I love you, too." I did. No matter what, she was my mum.

The call went dead.

"What did you say to him?"

"Basically, I told him he was an idiot if he did not start caring about his daughter, and stop acting like a douche, and I threatened to never let him near his grandkids if he didn't grow up and stop playing around."

Justin leaned forward and then pushed back, as the oars cut through the water.

"I think I got you wrong, Justin Preston, when I first knew

you… Thank you…"

A broad grin cut into his face. "Well, I had you down for being someone entirely different. But then I saw you, just you, and I was hooked."

He leaned forward again and before he could pull back, I gripped his shoulders and hugged him hard. "Just you, is everything I want. I never thought that I would be this happy…"

"Nor me." His lips brushed my cheek with a kiss as I let him go.

"I want to go home and watch Disney films after this…"

He laughed…

Bonus Material

Book one in The Starting Out Series, I Found You, featured Jason and Rachel. Their story will continue throughout the next books in the series.

'Portia, look who just walked in.' I emailed her, then stood up, and saw her turn to look as I looked across the desks.

Jason was here. The guy who'd worked here until New Year. I'd not seen or heard from him since he'd walked out, the day Portia had been dying with embarrassment 'cause she didn't know what had happened in Mr. Rees's pool.

Jason looked agitated, angry and nervous, as he walked across the room, hands in the pockets of his brown leather jacket. But he had a determined stride. He hadn't looked my way but I presumed he'd come back to say hi.

"Jason!" I called as I walked 'round the desks to block his path. Portia was standing too, and the other girls were getting up. "Hey!"

He looked at me. His hands slipping out of his pockets but there wasn't really any pleasure in his eyes.

He did stop when he got close and let out a sigh. "Hey." It was like the welcome was grudging.

"What's up?" I couldn't keep the excitement out of my voice. I was pleased to see him. We'd been friends, I'd thought, except the mother-fucker had never answered a single text or call since he'd gone. Walking closer, I held out my hand. He took it, but he only held it for a moment then let go.

"How's your girl? How's the baby? Is it born?"

His gaze focused on me. "Yeah. It's a boy. He's called, Saint. He's doing good. But I've come in to see Mr. Rees. I need to ask him something."

"Yeah." That had my eyebrows lifting.

Portia stepped forward making her presence known, in full Miss-perfect in-office mode. That was the Portia Jason had known, and he hadn't liked her, no matter how much she'd tried to make him. She pressed against my side, and I tucked my arm around her as she held her hand out.

"Justin and I are engaged."

Jason's eyes widened as he looked from her to me. "*Really*?" I'd given *him* a lot of shit about doing things too fast when he'd got engaged.

"Yeah." *Really.* "When you know something's right… You don't wait. You know that, Jason…"

His lips shifted into a lopsided smile. I could see he wasn't convinced Portia was *right* for me, but he didn't know the Portia I did.

"Well, whatever. Good Luck. I've got to go talk to Mr. Rees. Then I'm out of here."

"Yeah. Okay. But say good-bye when you come out, and keep in touch this time."

He just shrugged. I didn't think he would.

Portia looked at me when he walked away and then once we saw him disappear into Mr. Rees's office, we followed. I could see Jason leaning over Mr. Rees's desk through a glass panel in the door. No one did that unless they had a suicide wish, but then Jason wasn't working here anymore. But if he wanted a reference, that wasn't the way to get it.

Portia and I stood a couple of yards from the office, opening

154

our mouths like we were talking quietly, saying nothing, so we could hear.

"I'm tired of your fucking games," Jason was saying. "Just do it, you want this to get swept away, and I want the same thing, but I want it done right. Just do the damn test and then either way, you'll get rid. Okay! Here!"

I could see Jason slide something across the table, a small packet. Mr. Rees looked up. I looked at Portia.

I couldn't hear Mr. Rees's answer, he wasn't shouting. But he looked angry as hell when I glanced back.

"Yeah. Well. We'll see. But if you are, then I want you to sign the papers or I'll be back. Then... This won't go away! I'll drag you through every fucking court there is!"

The office door was thrust open again and Jason came out, red in the face, and looking as if he'd have steam coming out his ears if cartoons were real.

Portia moved forward but I stuck out a hand and held her back, then followed him alone. When I caught up with him, I said quietly, "Problems?"

He didn't slow down but glanced at me. "You could say that, but it's nothing for you to give a shit about. Just keep it quiet."

"I can keep things as silent as the grave..."

He finally smiled. "Justin, that is not you. You and Portia are probably the perfect match. Gossips."

"Well, I discovered she is pretty perfect when you know her, gossip or not."

He smiled at me fully then, we were still walking, but he slapped a hand on my shoulder. "I'm happy for you."

"Thanks. Same."

When we got to the door at the end of the floor, he turned and gripped my shoulder harder. "It's good to see you. But I'm not keeping in touch. My life's kind of moved on."

"Yeah?"

"In a good way, Justin."

His life had pivoted around the girl he'd met last year. Mine now pivoted around Portia. "I got it."

Portia was everything...

Read on for an exclusive sneak peek at chapter one of I Found You.

Chapter One

The beat of the music pounded through my earphones, drowning out the loud rattle of the subway trains. I was in the zone. My heart was racing, my feet striking the pavement with the rhythm of the bassline as I ran.

The monotony of city life swamped me in the day, but running brought me back from it at night.

God, I missed home, and fuck it was cold.

Too cold to snow. I heard the words Dad always repeated. I'd always thought it a myth. Was it ever too cold to snow? I didn't know, but people had been saying it all day.

The pavement was dry, not icy. Dry with cold. There was no moisture in the air, only the cloud of my breath, as my lungs filled and then exhaled with the pace of my strides.

Maybe it was true. God, there were so many myths in the world. Like, New York City was the place to be. It still felt like new shoes to me, like it just didn't fit.

The asphalt felt firm beneath my sneakers.

I looked forward, trying to increase my pace and energy, burning away the doubts and disappointments I'd felt since I came to the city.

At the end of the bridge there was a figure, caught in the middle of a beam of orange lamplight, like some illuminated angel. I

157

generally only saw other guys jogging on the bridge path. It was rare to see anyone else.

It was Thanksgiving in little over a week and Christmas in a few weeks. Lindy was pissed I wasn't going back home, but she'd made up her mind to come to me for Christmas.

Was that good or bad?

The figure was facing the Brooklyn Bridge, probably looking at the reflection of the lights glinting and shifting on the dark water. It was mesmerizing when you focused on it.

The Manhattan Bridge was never busy, probably because of the noise of the trains. The environment didn't inspire pleasure, so it wasn't a place for tourists. But it was a good path for running: long and straight, and normally empty.

I ran harder, my eyes focusing on the figure.

The person hadn't moved. They held their hands up, gripping the metal grill above them.

The pose seemed odd. A little desperate. It wasn't casual.

My imagination shifted, no longer picturing angels but a horror movie. The way the lamplight shone down on the figure was like they were in the sights of a hovering helicopter, or a beam from a UFO.

I thought of Christmas again, and ached for home. But I wasn't going home. I had to conquer New York.

The light shining down on the stranger suddenly took the form of a Godly benediction once more. The person's arms shifted, stretching out, similar to a crucifixion pose, hands wide and high as they looked upward.

I was getting nearer.

My fingers were numb with the cold, even inside my gloves, and my ears burned as the frost nipped beneath my hood. Running should've kept me warm, but it was twenty-one degrees Fahrenheit, way below freezing point.

Fuck, now I could see the person ahead was standing in a t-shirt. Their outstretched arms were bare.

"Hey!" My heart rate thundered as I ran on, wondering what sort of sketchy city-nutter I was running toward. What were they doing wearing a tee in this weather? It didn't look like a homeless dude, but…

My breaths grew more uneven.

The guy ahead hadn't heard me.

I pulled my earphones out. "Hey!"

Still no recognition. It was like they were in some sort of trance.

My feet pounded on the concrete.

It wasn't a guy, it was a girl. I'd seen the long hair way back, but hadn't been sure. Plenty of guys had long hair. But now, I could see.

I knocked my hood back. I didn't want to scare her. "Hey!"

Nothing. Not a single sign of recognition and I was only yards away. She was wearing skinny jeans and sneakers with her tee.

Her hands moved, catching hold of the wire like she was going to climb it, then her foot lifted, seeking a grip on the railing.

Her arms bracing her weight; her other foot lifted. What the hell was she doing? Trying to go over the wire? Did she want to jump?

"Hey! Wait!"

I ran harder.

Fuck. She looked serious and she carried on climbing, searching out hand and foot holds.

"Are you crazy? Stop it!"

As I ran the last few yards her gaze finally turned to me. I covered the distance in moments, watching her clinging on the wire, Spiderman style.

God knows what she saw in my eyes. I could see nothing in hers except maybe fear. They were huge, and dark, staring at me like I was the weird one.

I wasn't the weird one.

My music continued playing muted sounds and air rasped into my lungs as I stopped. I lifted a hand, palm up, offering to help her down. "Come on…" My breath fogged the air around us. "Nothing's that bad…"

159

She held still. Her eyes had no depth. It was like looking into mirrors, reflecting back the electric light. She looked a little mad.

"Let me help you."

She was panting as hard as I was. She didn't come down.

She was only a couple of feet off the floor, I could pull her down, but I didn't want to scare her.

My fingers instinctively lifted and touched her lower back. I could feel the breath pulling into her lungs. "Look, seriously, you don't want to do anything foolish."

She didn't move.

"What's your name?" Shit. My heart was still racing like I was running. I looked along the bridge path, but there was no one else here to help.

"Honey, come on down. I can't let you do it."

She was just staring at me.

What the hell did cops say to persuade a person…? "You must be cold, you can have my hoodie. I'm not going to leave you here."

This was like some TV drama.

My hands were trembling from the blood burning in my muscles. I'd gone from running hard to standing still. A weight of responsibility fell on me suddenly. This girl's life was in my hands. I'd been running wrapped up in my own world and now… Shit. "Really. Please… Come down."

Pleading obviously touched some nerve in her, as one foot came back down onto the concrete, her cotton t-shirt catching on my glove and crumpling up, revealing the pale skin of her lower back. My gaze dropped to her plain white sneakers, as the next foot touched the ground.

Relief washed through me on a wave as I lifted my hand so her t-shirt slid back down. I looked up and met her gaze. It was still blank though, and her fingers gripped the wire.

I touched her shoulder. It lifted as air pulled into her lungs, before slipping back out. I didn't know why I was touching her, but I just… I needed to know she was okay. She didn't seem to know where she was, or what she'd been doing.

A dark smear marked her face, and whatever it was, it stained her hair too.

Every sermon I'd endured as a kid raced through my head. Help the needy; put others first; don't walk past that mugged guy in the street. I hadn't gone to church for years, not since I'd hit my teens, but religion was stitched into my DNA. No way could I walk past a person in need.

My shock dissipating, I stripped off my hoodie. The smell of my sweat permeated the cold air. She probably wouldn't want it but she needed it. "How long have you been up here? It's freezing." She could have been up here half an hour. She hadn't been here when I'd run over the bridge into Manhattan.

For a minute I didn't think she'd take it, but then her hand reached out. "I don't know?"

"You know it's twenty-one degrees Fahrenheit, right? You'll get hyperthermia." She looked at me, her eyes still dead. "I'm Jason... Were you trying to do what I thought?"

She didn't answer.

I held out my hand. "Hi."

She didn't shake my hand, just looked at it.

"Look, nothing can be that bad. You'll get over it, and be glad you didn't jump."

"Will I?" Her pitch was mocking, although maybe she was mocking her own thoughts, not my words, nothing in her eyes or her face told me though.

What now? I could hardly just run on and leave her here. Dammit. "I..." I could take her to emergency... What would they do? Check her over and spit her out. "Have you got any family locally?"

"No."

"Friends?"

"No."

Her large eyes confirmed what she'd said. She had nowhere to

161

go. Her full lips pouted a little. Shit. What did I do?

"Where do you live then? Is there somewhere I can take you?"

She was pretty. Her face glowed in the electric light, showing a clear complexion and perfectly even features, though her skin was yellowish in this light.

"No. Nowhere."

Why was she here? What had made her life too hard to carry on?

She shivered, and pain etched its expression on her face, then tears suddenly glittered in her eyes, and the coldness in them became a lake of desolation. "I need to get away."

"From what?"

She didn't answer, but her teeth started chattering. I lifted the hood of my sweatshirt over her blonde hair.

"Look, obviously things aren't okay for you. What are you going to do?"

"I don't know."

I took a breath, looking at her and hoping some magical solution would suddenly hit me. It didn't, and I was getting cold now.

She shivered again and her arms crossed, her hands gripping the opposite elbows. She'd stopped looking at me. She was looking at the sky, like she was searching for answers too.

I sighed, my fingers running over my hair. She was nearly as tall as me, and I was six foot one. She must be at least five eight. But she was slender, like a model. My sweatshirt swamped her figure. She looked fragile.

Shit. There was nothing I could do. "What are you going to do, if I go?"

Her shoulders lifted in a shrug, but she didn't look down.

My heart was thumping to the same rhythm as the bass beat now pounding out of the earphones dangling 'round my neck

I couldn't leave her out here...

"Have you really got nowhere to go?"

She shook her head, making her blonde ponytail sweep over her back.

Shit. What option did I have? What option did she have?

"Have you got any money?"

Her head shook again. But her stillness, apart from her shaking head, made me feel like she didn't even care. I felt stupid then, of course she didn't care. She'd just tried to end her life by throwing herself off a bridge. She obviously didn't care about anything right now.

What to do with her? I could give her money... But I'd have to go back to my apartment to get my card and take her to a cash dispenser. And what would she do with it? Maybe she'd already taken something. Drugs or drink. Maybe that was why she was so dead looking. I'd be stupid to give her money.

I sighed again. I could call the cops and take her to a station. But what would they care? *I found this girl and she's got nowhere to stay.* They'd say, yeah, right, join the line of a couple of hundred other homeless people in New York.

There wasn't any choice. "I could take you home with me, if you've got nowhere to go. Just for tonight. It would give you chance to get your head straight, and get warm. If you want?"

"I..." She looked at me again then, her eyes losing their depth once more and setting up shutters, locking me out.

"What do you think?" I got another shrug, but her eyes suddenly filled with depth, letting me see into the thoughts behind her gaze. They were asking me questions.

"What are you going to do if you don't come back with me?" Another shrug. "Have you got any other options?" She shook her head, her ponytail swaying, but her gaze was clinging to mine now, like was she was considering me. Maybe she was trying to judge if she'd be safe.

This was surreal, like I'd been lifted out of real life, and placed in the middle of a fucking film. Question was; how was it going to play out? Taking her home was a risk, but sometimes risks had to be taken. Like coming to New York.

I sighed again. Sometimes taking risks didn't pay off. But I still hoped they would.

She shivered and her hands gripped her arms harder.

I lifted my hands palm outward. "I swear. I'm the nice guy. And if you've got nowhere else to go…" Lindy would go mad, but this was devil or deep-blue-sea territory. How could I leave this woman here? She'd nowhere to sleep and it was twenty-one degrees Fahrenheit.

Her shoulders shook as she shivered again.

"It's not far. I live in DUMBO."

"Down under the Manhattan Bridge Overpass…" she whispered. "It's such a cool name for a neighborhood."

I laughed. She didn't.

"Have you got any other choice?"

She shook her head.

"Then on my life, if you come, I'll not hurt you."

She said nothing just looked at me.

"My apartment's warm. You can't stay out here…" Shit, I was probably just as crazy as her, offering to take a stranger back with me.

"I…"

"I swear, you're safe with me."

She looked back at the wire, then down at the water.

"You don't want to do that. Just give it a night, you'll feel different in the morning."

She shook her head, still looking at the water.

If zombies were real, they'd look like her. My sweatshirt swamping her, she stood like a sorrowful statue, her complexion as pale as marble.

I couldn't just leave her. I rubbed her arms, gently, answering an instinct to put my arm around her, but I denied that. I didn't even know her name.

"Look, you can trust me. Honest. When we get back to my apartment you can call my Mom, or my friends, and they'll all tell you I'm the nice guy. Seriously, if you need references…" I

164

smiled as she looked back at me, trying to convince her. "What do you say? Are you a gambler? Are you going to try trusting me?" Silence and stillness. This girl was messed up. But then I'd known that from the moment I'd seen her. She'd been standing in the freezing cold, in a tee, trying to jump off a bridge.

I held her gaze, trying to look inside her, as she looked back, trying to see inside me.

Once more there was a sudden pool of desolation and a glitter in her eyes, and she simply nodded, making the choice to put herself into the hands of a stranger—my hands.

Shit. *I was taking her home.* She could be a drug addict. I'd been so busy trying to persuade her, I'd forgotten about my own concerns. But I couldn't leave her here alone; fragility and loneliness rang from her, like she was crying out for help. And the damned Good Samaritan story I'd been brought up on wouldn't let me leave her in the street.

But what the hell was I getting myself into?

"This way." My fingers carefully closed about her upper arm, and I guided her to turn and start walking off the bridge with me, like this was a normal thing to do—like every night of the week, I took a stranger home. My guts churned. This was crazy. But my fingers wrapped right about her skinny arm, and my instincts yelled at me that she needed protecting, and she needed safety. I could let her have a haven for a few days.

She was probably a size zero, she was so skinny.

Lindy would kill to be size zero. She would hate me taking this woman home. She wasn't flooded with human kindness. She wouldn't have felt any instinct to help this woman.

"You haven't told me your name yet?" I prodded as we descended the steps onto the street.

She was moving robotically. I was a stranger to her, too, and she hadn't questioned me verbally at all. She was going home with a guy she didn't know.

Maybe she did this all the time.

Maybe her lack of concern should warn me off.

As if sensing my thoughts, she stopped and looked at me, hard, really looking into me, like she'd done on the bridge just now, maybe at last deciding she ought to check me out a little more. "It's Rachel."

"Rachel—pleased to meet you. My apartment's in a block near here, it's not far. You're sure about this, yeah? I could still take you somewhere else, if you like?"

"I've got nowhere else to go. So I haven't got any choice. You don't mind?"

I do, really, but I'm not mean enough to dump you here. "No, I don't mind."

I pressed my code in when we reached the building, feeling guilty for covering it up, showing I didn't trust her, but I didn't know her.

"My furniture's a bit sparse at the moment. I only just moved in a couple of months back. Don't expect anything fancy…" We entered the elevator and I pressed the button. "I'm on the fifth floor." That was obvious, the red light behind button five glowed, announcing it.

I turned and looked at her. What I'd thought was dirt on her face and in her hair, was dried blood. "Did you hit your head?"

Her gaze struck mine, questioning and cold, and in the white light of the elevator, I faced green eyes. They were a misty green, an unusual sort of green. I'd never seen that eye color before. She didn't answer me though. She hadn't spoken since she'd given me her name, and her fingers were curled up, hidden in the sleeves of my sweatshirt, as her arms gripped across her chest.

She looked down at my Adam's apple.

"You don't have to be worried."

Those green eyes looked up again. "I'm not scared of you. You gave me your hoodie. People who are generally mean, don't give you stuff they need themselves."

It was an odd, but reasonable, logic. "Yeah, well…." I didn't know what to say, yet all my friends in Oregon would say I was never lost for words. "Okay."

The elevator bell rang, announcing that we'd reached the fifth floor, and then the doors opened.

I looked away from her. She was a little too beautiful for comfort. She had untouchable celeb-magazine beauty, the sort you knew you'd never have, so you never wanted. Lindy was pretty, but there was a quality of perfection in this Rachel. Yet she wasn't perfect was she, or her life wasn't, she'd been trying to jump off Manhattan Bridge.

I wanted to know what led her there, but I wasn't going to make her feel like I was prying, I didn't ask.

I pulled the key from the pocket of my joggers, unlocked the door and stepped back to let her go first, flicking the lights on.

"Chivalrous to a fault…" she whispered. "Do you stand up for pregnant and elderly women on subway trains?"

Actually I did. Lindy always said I was a dying breed. Mom always took credit. "And sometimes I even carry their shopping back."

She looked at me again. "You don't come from New York do you? Are you some hillbilly?"

"I'm from Oregon, from a small town there."

"Out of college and flying the nest…"

She sounded like she was laughing at me, but there was no humor in her face or her eyes. What I saw was grief.

"Do you want some coffee, I can make a pot? It'll warm you up." I took her fingers. I could feel how cold they were even through my gloves. They were like blocks of ice. I rubbed them for a moment.

Her hands fell when I let them go.

I felt awkward, but the only thing to do now I'd brought her back here, was to act like I was completely comfortable with it.

I took off my gloves. They were damp. How'd they get damp?

There was no life in her eyes, once more, when her gaze met mine.

She turned and looked about the room. It was empty bar my TV, my Xbox and a beanbag.

I left her and went to make coffee. The kitchen was to one side of the living space.

"The bathroom's through there, if you need it?" I pointed to the door leading into my bedroom. "There's only one bed, or rather one mattress, I don't own a bed. But you can have it tonight. I'll manage on the floor in here."

Those pale green eyes turned to me again. "You're too nice, Jason…?" Her pitch asked for my surname.

"Macinlay."

"You've Irish blood?"

"Two generations ago. Dad's been back there once, kissed the Blarney Stone, driven the Ring of Kerry and stepped on the Giant's Causeway."

She smiled, but it was shallow. Yet I guessed she was doing her best to push aside the awkwardness of this too. "I have no reason to trust you, Jason Macinlay," she breathed, "but I do."

Again, I didn't know what to say. I just shrugged.

I'd left the bedroom door ajar; she pushed it wider and went through, her hand slipping off it, leaving a blood mark.

Fuck. "What did you do to your hand?" I was moving before I knew and she stopped and turned, but took a step away from me into the bedroom when I neared. "Don't tell me you had a go at your wrists, too…" I gripped her forearm.

She had nowhere to run to in my bedroom. You could barely swing a cat in it. There was about a foot of space all around the double mattress which lay on the floor.

I pulled up the sleeve of the sweatshirt I'd given her.

Her wrists were narrow. They looked so fucking breakable. But they weren't slashed. The blood had come from a jagged cut across her palm. It didn't look like it had been done by a knife, and the blood had begun congealing.

I glanced at her fingers. I'd heard people injected heroin beneath their fingernails to hide the marks. There were no marks on her arms, and there seemed to be none under her nails. It was probably safe to guess her problem wasn't heroin.

"How did you do it?" I'd been avoiding questions, I figured she wouldn't speak, but I couldn't help myself now. "What happened?"

She shrugged, letting my question slide away, as she'd been doing on the bridge. Her gaze, which had been looking at her hand too, lifted to me, but she said nothing.

I let her hand go. "Why don't you run a bath? You can talk when you want."

The cold had probably stopped her losing too much blood. "Don't get your hand in the water, though."

"What are you, a nurse?" There was that mocking pitch in her voice again.

"No, I work for a magazine."

"And from your voice, you don't like it?"

"Not at the moment, and I don't like the city either. I'm new to it."

"Well, I'm not. Maybe I can help you in return, then, seeing as you're helping me."

I didn't want to give her any expectations, we weren't friends. "You need to just get warm first."

She turned away.

Jason Macinlay wasn't like any man I'd known. He was considerate. I didn't know what to make of him. I'd met guys on the street before, but when they'd taken me back to their place, it hadn't been to get me out of the cold.

His place was minimalistic and his bedcovers were crumpled and thrown back. Yet he wasn't untidy. It just suggested he took life as he found it. Like he didn't need order.

I looked at the doors.

The first one I opened was a closet. It contained rough heaps of his clothing. The second was the bathroom.

I turned the water on and touched it with my bloody hand. A stinging pain burned in my palm. I must have left blood on the doors. I looked at the gash as blood dripped into the water. The warmth had made it bleed again. I saw the scarlet ribbons of blood spinning in the white porcelain sink back at Declan's.

I didn't want to think about how I'd cut it. I shut that out. I'd ended it. I was starting over. I had to find a job, find a life— somewhere to live.

I used the toilet as the water ran, and held the neck of Jason Macinlay's sweaty top up to my nose. The fresh male musky scent was ridiculously comforting. I breathed it in. There was something about him that made me feel safer than I'd felt in an entire year, or maybe longer. Nothing in his eyes had said he'd brought me back here because he wanted sex. He'd said he was *a nice guy*. Those words were still swimming around in my muddled head.

Was I going mad again? Had I really injured Declan? My eyes shut for a moment as images whisked through my brain and swept away. I couldn't grasp hold of them. I didn't want to. I just wanted to get away.

But I *had* got away. I'd gotten here. I had nowhere else to go.

I was suddenly very aware of the pace of my breathing. It felt too fast. I remembered seeing people breathing into paper bags when they hyperventilated and focused on breathing in the same way, trying to slow it down. I stripped off Jason Macinlay's top, then my t-shirt. Then I took off my sneakers and jeans.

I hadn't put on any underwear in my haste to get out.

I got into the water. It was really warm and the heat absorbed all my pain, physical and mental.

Pictures of the black water I'd seen beneath the bridge, swelling and rocking, played through my mind. I imagined it absorbing me, a great dark, thick, fluid weight.

It would be so much easier to slip beneath the water. I didn't have the courage or the strength to go on. How could I begin again?

A knock struck the bathroom door. Then it opened. Jason

Macinlay walked in.

"Shit, sorry... You should've shouted." His eyes skimmed over my body before he turned his back. He wasn't so saintly then.

I sat up, the water swilling around me. "It's just a body. You must've seen a hundred naked women." He was too good-looking to be inhibited, surely. He'd probably had tons of women in his bed.

"I brought your coffee."

"Yeah, I guessed."

He held it out, without turning. He felt awkward about me being here, I'd seen that the minute we'd got to his front door. I knew what it was like to sleep on the streets, though, and he was right, it was freezing. But what I'd said to him in the elevator was true. I trusted him. Probably more than I'd trusted any other guy—no one had given me their sweaty top before, when I was cold.

I took the cup from him, and put it on the lip of the tub. Blood dripped into the water. "My hand's bleeding." It was shaking too.

He looked across his shoulder, at my hand, nothing else. "I'll find something. I've got a first-aid kit. There should be a bandage in there." He went again.

The cocaine I'd taken with Declan was still spinning through my nerves and my heartbeat lifted my breasts a little as it thumped, while my damp hair brushed the skin on my back and shoulders. I had a sense of déjà-vu, though I could never have been here before. But it was like I was meant to come to this place.

I picked up the coffee with my left hand, my good hand, and sipped from it. Warmth ran into my blood. The cold had got deep inside me.

"I turned the heating up," Jason said, as he came back in. "Do you want to pull the shower curtain and just stick your hand out."

I looked up at him and met his deep brown gaze.

He had large eyes, strong features, and broad lips, and his dark brown hair was cut close to his head but it wasn't gelled.

He looked good. He'd probably broken a few girls' hearts back in Oregon.

171

I didn't bother with the shower curtain, I held out my hand as his gaze clung to my face, like he was trying desperately not to look down.

He needn't worry. I was used to being naked with men. My body was just flesh and bone. I knew he wanted to look down, all men wanted to look, it was in their nature. Well, unless it wasn't women they were into.

With a deep sigh his gaze fell to my hand as he gripped it. "Okay, I mixed boiled water with the antiseptic so it'll take a moment to cool."

He put the lid of the toilet down and sat on it, holding my hand and looking at the gash.

I couldn't imagine Declan ever doing anything like this. He'd have told me to fucking get on with it and stop moaning.

But I hadn't moaned had I? Jason Macinlay had seen the blood and asked about it. I shouldn't feel guilty then that he was helping. But I did. This was my own fault. *I* should be fixing it.

"It could need stitches."

"I'm not going to a hospital. I can't stand those places. I'll be fine."

I took my hand from his and he looked up, his gaze caught on my breasts then lifted.

See, a man, he couldn't help but look.

He met my gaze, and I knew he knew I'd seen him look. There was color in his cheeks. It made me want to laugh. He didn't look like he'd had that many women when he blushed, but he was gorgeous, surely he must have had a few.

His brown gaze held mine. "Okay, no hospital."

I gave him my hand again.

His touch was really gentle for a man. I bent up my knees in the tub and wrapped my other arm about them, watching him. He had some antiseptic in a cup and dunked cotton-wool pads into it, then wiped the blood from my hand, while he rested the back of it on his knee.

I couldn't remember anyone ever paying so much attention to one of my hurts. "Did your mom do this for you when you were a boy; is that how you learned to treat wounds?"

His brown eyes looked up and said he didn't appreciate the comment.

"Have you got a big family then, back in the hills?"

"The hills?" His eyebrows lifted, and then he answered in a dry tone. "Very funny... I didn't grow up in the middle of nowhere, you know. It's a small town, not a shack."

"With a small town society and small town views—"

"And moms who teach you how to clean a wound if you get injured... What's so bad about that?"

"Nothing..."

His brown eyes looked hard at me for a moment. But those eyes were easy to look at, and he had long dark, almost feminine, eyelashes.

"Right. So just let me get on with it, Rachel..." His gaze fell to my hand again, then after a moment he glanced back up. "Do you have a family somewhere?"

Yes, but not that I cared to speak of. I felt my lips compress.

His eyes hovered on mine for a moment, asking unspoken questions, before they dropped to look at my hand once more.

His touch was caring, as well as gentle.

He looked up and saw me watching, then smiled, suddenly. He had a nice smile too, a really open-hearted smile.

This was a genuine guy. Someone like Declan would eat him alive. "So you don't like your job?"

"I don't know. There's so much frigging office politics, I can't keep up with it. I think I need to be a bit more cutthroat, but I'm not that type. I can't be bothered with all the backstabbing, and I have an asshole for a boss. So I spent three years in college, and now I'm the office nobody."

Yeah, Declan would definitely eat him alive.

"Talk to me about it. I can teach you backstabbing..." I shouldn't

173

have said that, the image and sound of the mirror splintering pierced my mind, and I felt the shard gripped in my hand as it sank into Declan's flesh.

I felt sick. I let my forehead drop onto my knees, while my hand still rested in Jason Macinlay's secure grip, and my arm hung outstretched to him. My other hugged my knees.

"Where do you come from, Rachel…?" he prodded a moment later, as though he was sweeping the previous topic under a rug and moving on.

His hesitation asked my last name, I'd give him that, but nothing more. "Shears. My name is Rachel Shears." I looked up again, as my lips compressed.

His brown eyes looked hard into mine, but he didn't push for more.

He looked down at my hand. "It's clean. I'll bandage it up."

When he let it go, I left my hand lying on his knee. His legs were parted and his sweatpants were loose, but his top was tight, it hugged his abs and the pectoral muscles of his chest as he leaned to the side and picked up a bandage from the first-aid box.

He was beautiful, but unlike Declan there seemed to be beauty inside him too, it wasn't just a surface thing. He was helping me.

I wanted to turn my hand and grip his thigh. But that would be the wrong thing to do. I knew that. But I was really good at doing wrong things.

Voices inside me encouraged me to do it. I didn't. The cocaine was still clouding my view.

He straightened and his fingers gripped the back of my hand more firmly. It sent tremors running up the nerves in my arm.

His other hand laid the bandage over my palm and his thumb pressed down on the dressing he'd used to cover my cut, securing it, then he began winding the bandage round my hand.

I shut my eyes.

His touch was doing stuff in my belly, making it clasp with need. I wanted sex. I hadn't wanted it with Declan anymore, but

174

I wanted it with Jason Macinlay. Sex was the best escape from the things going on in my head. It had never even really mattered who I did it with. I just liked it, and I'd always found a guy who'd give me a place to stay in return for it. They just generally weren't the right guys.

I'd never even liked Declan. And the feeling had been mutual. But we'd connected in bed. He liked things wild, and wild played to my crazy. God, had I really done that stuff with him? I needed something better now.

I opened my eyes and watched Jason Macinlay concentrating. He wound the bandage round and round, pulling it tight to stop the blood; watching what he was doing, not watching me.

I felt hot, and the tingle in my tummy slid to the point between my legs. I was sitting naked in a tub beside this guy. When had I decided to undress? I didn't know him. Really, my head was stupid.

Yes I did, he was Jason Macinlay, from Oregon, and he'd already given me more respect than Declan had done in the last year.

"How old are you?" I asked.

His brown eyes lifted and met my gaze again.

He was feeling more relaxed, I could tell, his breathing seemed more normal and his muscles less tense.

"Twenty-two. You?"

"Twenty-one."

"That's too young to want to end your life, Rachel Shears."

I shrugged, my lips compressing.

Of course he wanted to know why I'd been there, but I didn't want to talk and I couldn't remember half of it anyway. His eyes said, 'what happened?' I didn't answer.

He smiled, not his stunning smile of a few moments ago, but a closed lip smile that said, okay, so you don't wanna talk, I understand.

No one understood me. I'd learned that the hard way.

Mom would've said she did, when I was a kid. She didn't, and I hadn't even seen her in years. I didn't even know why I was

175

thinking of her today. I hadn't thought of her in months. I hadn't spoken to her since I was fifteen.

Maybe I was thinking of her because I wished she'd been a proper mom and had taught me how to clean a wound like Jason Macinlay.

"Drink your coffee, and don't get that in the water." He stood up, letting my hand go.

I reached for the mug of coffee with my good hand. It was already lukewarm, like the water. I started to feel cold again, and shivered.

"Run some more hot water. I'll leave you to it."

He walked out then, and left me, shutting the door behind him.

I used my bandaged hand to turn the water on.

The bandage was neat and tight.

I lay back in the water, and let the heat seep into me. But it wasn't just the warmth of the water which was penetrating my body. I could fall for this guy, Jason Macinlay. That was another thing I was good at, jumping from one guy to another. It was what I did best.

~

"Hey,"

"Yeah, I know it's late. I'm sorry, I…"

I woke in bed, hearing Jason Macinlay whispering in the room next door.

He'd changed the covers on the mattress while I'd bathed. The sheet and duvet cover smelt fresh and felt crisp.

I'd rather he'd left the old sheets on, it would have felt more comforting. I'd missed his scent from his sweatshirt. He'd thrown that in the washer, too, like I'd marked it and he needed to wash me off it.

Declan must have washed all the blood off by now, mine and his. I was gone from his life. That poisonous relationship was over.

"Something happened, Lindy. I couldn't call earlier. But I'm calling now."

The door was shut between the bedroom and the living space.

"Yeah, I know."

I rolled over and listened more intently, I could even hear him breathing between the words.

He sounded defensive.

"Look…" The pitch of his voice dropped. "I found a girl on Manhattan Bridge, Lind. She was trying to jump. I couldn't just leave her."

There was silence for a moment as he breathed. I imagined this Lindy speaking at the other end.

"I brought her home."

Silence.

"Yeah, well, I didn't know what else to do."

"Lindy, leave it, she's no risk."

"I'll be fine."

"Yeah, honest, I'll take care. I can look out for myself."

"I know this is New York."

"Yeah, right."

"Look, I'm going to go. I don't want to wake her."

"She's sleeping in my bed. I'm sleeping on the floor."

"She won't."

"I won't."

"Look Lindy, I'll call you tomorrow, normal time. I'm going to go now, and don't worry."

"Yeah, I love you, too."

"Yeah, tomorrow." He sighed, like he had the weight of the world on his shoulders.

I needed a drink. I threw the covers back and got up, then knocked on the door leading back into the living space.

He didn't answer; he couldn't have heard, but I didn't like to just walk in. I knocked more loudly.

"Yeah?"

"You decent?"

He laughed. It was low and heavy. "Yeah."

I opened the door.

He was sitting on the floor, gilded by the moonlight streaming through a floor to ceiling window which lit his living room. His arms were about his knees as one hand still gripped his cell and his head was bent a little forward.

He looked defeated.

"Sorry." I didn't even know why I apologized, I just felt as if I was intruding.

"It's alright. Did I wake you? Sorry."

"I want some water." I moved to the kitchen counter and watched him as I ran it, waiting for it to run cool. He was wearing a loose t-shirt now, with boxers. His forearms and his shins were dusted with dark hair. I could see it even in the blue-black light in the room.

The clock on the TV flashed eleven-thirty. I didn't feel as though I'd get back to sleep, and my hand was hurting like hell now; it was throbbing with the beat of my heart.

"Is she your girlfriend?"

"Lindy? Yeah."

"She's back in Oregon?"

"Yeah."

"Bet she feels small town, now you've gone all big city."

"Ha. Ha." His pitch was dismissive. Life clearly wasn't all roses between them.

"I suppose you've been with her forever. What was she, the head of the cheerleaders while you captained the football team?"

"You think you know me so well, don't you..."

He *had* been captain of the football team.

I bet they were best looking girl and best looking boy in their year, and they'd gotten together because it was what everyone expected.

"I was the kid who sat in the corner and never had friends..."

I didn't know why I told him that, I just thought it might make him feel better.

"And now?"

My lips compressed.

Turning away, I opened a cupboard and found a glass. "Do you want a drink?"

"No thanks."

I filled the glass and drank, as again the images of the mirror breaking disturbed my thoughts.

I pushed the memory away. I was starting over and forgetting that.

I moved about the counter, and leaned back against it, facing him. "So what's wrong between you?"

"Tonight? You. She thinks you're going to either jump me in my sleep, or steal all my stuff, like I have anything worth stealing." His hand lifted and swept forward indicating the virtually empty room.

"She might be right, though?" I did feel like jumping him in his sleep. It would be a great way to escape the blackness which kept threatening to swamp me.

His gaze focused up at me as he scanned my face. "She could be right, yes…"

Well, he didn't know me, and I'd said nothing about myself, bar my name and my age. "She isn't. You're safe."

"Phew, thank fuck for that."

I laughed. He was a nice guy. There weren't many of those in the world. I wasn't used to them.

My eyes shifted to the white pillow on the hard floor behind him. Then I looked at him again.

"So anyway, seeing as I've promised not to jump you in your sleep, why don't you share the mattress? If you're safe, it seems silly you trying to sleep out here." I'd be good. He deserved for me to be good. He'd been kind to me.

He looked at me for a long moment. I didn't move, holding out against his assessment.

I wasn't blind. I knew he liked what he saw. I was wearing his t-shirt, my legs were bare, and I'd nothing on underneath. It would be so easy to be bad. His gaze ran up my legs and my body then came to my face. But he wasn't *that* sort of guy.

All men looked. It didn't mean all men let themselves touch.

"Yeah, okay, I won't get any sleep here anyway."

He picked up his pillow and stood, then lifted the pillow indicating for me to walk ahead.

I went into the bathroom, while he lay down on the mattress, under the covers.

When I came back in, he was watching me, one arm behind his head.

I said nothing, walked to the other side and got in.

He probably wouldn't mind if I jumped him, but he'd have a hell of a conscience the next day when he spoke to his Lindy.

I turned my back to him and felt him roll onto his stomach. My body was intensely aware of his, and all I could hear was his breathing as he drifted into sleep, while all I could smell was his shampoo, because he'd showered after I'd bathed.

This had been a weird day, I'd finally left Declan and within hours I'd acquired a stranger. My brain wasn't on the same page as where my life had gotten to. I'd walked out on the life of rich egotistical playboys, and into an opposite extreme.

An ex had once called me a parasite—maybe I was. But maybe I didn't want to be anymore.